THE SWISS FAMILY
ROBINSON

THE SWISS FAMILY ROBINSON

by

JOHANN R. WYSS

ABRIDGED

PRINTED IN   GREAT BRITAIN
DEAN & SON Ltd.
41/43 Ludgate Hill   LONDON EC4
TRADE MARK

MADE AND PRINTED IN GREAT BRITAIN BY PURNELL AND SONS LTD.,
PAULTON (AVON) AND LONDON

SBN 603 03037 8

CONTENTS

CHAPTER 1

Shipwreck, and Preparations for Deliverance

The tempest had lasted six days, and, far from abating, now redoubled in fury. Driven out of our course to the south-west, it was impossible to tell in what parts we were. Our vessel had lost her masts, and leaked from end to end.

"Children," I said to my four boys, who clung weeping to their mother, "God can still save if it be His will; if He has decreed otherwise we must submit. At the worst, we shall only quit this world to be united in the better one."

My wife dried her tears, and, following my example, assumed an enforced calmness, to inspire the children with courage and resignation.

All at once, through the roar of the winds and waters, I heard with rapture the salvation-cry of the shipwrecked—"Land! land!" But, at the same moment, we became sensible of a heavy concussion, succeeded by a frightful cracking noise. Thereupon, from the sudden cessation of motion in the ship, and the dull plash with which the waves broke around her, I concluded that we were stranded upon sunken rocks, and that the vessel was pierced through below.

"We are lost! Lower the boats!" cried a voice, which I recognised as that of the captain.

"Lost!" repeated the children, casting upon me a look full of anguish.

"Courage, my little ones!" I said, "despair not yet; God gives help to the brave. I will go and see what means can be taken for our safety."

I quitted the cabin, and went up on deck. Buffeted by the winds, half-blinded by the spray, flung down once or twice by the great seas that broke over the ship, I was unable for some moments to distinguish anything. When at length I reached the side, I saw the boats rocking among the waves, overcrowded with people, and obliged, for their safety, to stand out to sea.

A sailor was just cutting the last mooring rope.

We had been forgotten!

I shouted frantically, imploring them to return and save us; but my voice was lost in the roar of the storm, and I realised with horror that we were abandoned upon the wrecked vessel.

In my terrible extremity, however, I observed, with a feeling akin to consolation, that the ship had so grounded as to leave the poop, where our cabin was, thrust high up out of reach of the waves. And at the same time, even through the thick, misty rain which was falling, I could perceive, at some distance to the south, a coast-line that, in spite of its barren and desolate appearance, became thenceforward the object of my highest hopes.

I returned to my family, and, affecting a tranquillity which I was far from feeling:

"Take courage," said I, "all hope is not lost yet. One part of the ship is firmly fixed above the water. To-morrow the wind and waves will subside, and we shall be able to get to land."

From the manner in which my wife received my announcement, I saw clearly that she had penetrated the truth.

"We are about to pass a most distressing night," she said; "let us take some food. Nourishment for the body fortifies the soul."

Night fell. The tempest, in all its violence, continued to beat upon the vessel furiously. I feared every moment that she would break up.

My wife having hurriedly prepared a simple repast, the children partook of it with a good appetite. Then they retired to rest and slept soundly—all excepting Fritz, the eldest, who, comprehending the nature of our situation better than his brothers, chose to sit up with us.

"Father," he said, after a long interval of silence, "I have been trying to think of some means of reaching land. If we had either cork or bladders, to make swimming floats for mother and the other children, there would be no difficulty. You and I could swim ashore without help."

"A capital idea!" exclaimed I; "and that we may at all events be prepared, if the worst should come to the worst, let us try to put it in execution as soon as possible."

Having hunted up a number of empty kegs, and several of the tin cans in which persons at sea carry their daily allowance of fresh water, Fritz and I tied them in couples with our handkerchiefs, and fastened two under the armpits of my brave wife and each of the sleeping children. We also placed in their pockets and our own, knives, string, tinder-boxes, and other articles which we knew would be of prime necessity if the vessel should break up, and we be fortunate enough to reach the shore.

These precautions taken, Fritz, reassured and very much fatigued, went to bed as his brothers had done, and speedily fell asleep.

My wife and I continued our vigil.

With the first glimmerings of daylight I went up on deck. The wind was fast falling, the sea growing calm, and a lovely sunrise flashed its rose-tinted rays athwart a clear sky.

I called to my wife and my boys, who at once hastened up on deck.

The younger children were deeply concerned to see that we were alone on board.

"Where are the sailors?" they cried. "Why have they gone away without us? Oh, what is to become of us?"

"My children," said I, "our travelling companions were bewildered by fright. They leapt into the boats without thinking of us; and it is not unlikely that ere this they may have perished—victims of their own precipitation. If they still live I doubt not that they have more to complain of than we. See! the heavens are clear—land is not far off; our seeming misfortune, perhaps, is a blessing in disguise."

Fritz, enterprising and adventurous, persisted in his idea that it would be best to throw ourselves into the sea and swim to land.

"But," I said, "whatever we find ourselves compelled to do in the end, let us set about exploring the ship; so that while thinking upon the best means of reaching the land, we may gather upon deck everything that is likely to be of use to us when we get there."

Each hastened to do my bidding. I myself sought out the place where the provisions were stored, to make sure of what we had to depend upon for existence. Fritz visited the armoury and magazine, whence he brought guns, pistols, powder, balls and small shot. Ernest ransacked the carpenter's shop, and returned laden with tools and nails.

Little Francis—my youngest child, aged six—not to be outdone in activity, trotted about the vessel till he found a box full of fishhooks, which he showed us with much pride. Fritz and Ernest were inclined to make fun of him, but for my part I saw no reason to despise his discovery, for it might happen that we should be driven at last to live upon what fish we could catch, and then the hooks would be useful.

As to Jack—my third son, a merry youngster of ten years—he re-appeared with two huge dogs which he had found shut up in the captain's cabin, and which, rendered docile by hunger, allowed him to lead them each by the ear.

My wife came to tell me that she had found a cow, an ass, two she-goats, and a sow, and had given them food and water just in time to save their lives; for the poor animals had, in the confusion, been kept without nourishment of any kind for nearly two days.

Everybody appeared to me to have made some useful discovery, except Jack.

"My boy," I said, "you have found us a couple of terrible eaters which will consume much and provide nothing."

"I thought, dear father," he replied, "that they might be useful for hunting when we get to land."

"You are right," I said, "they might, but we have not yet got to land. Have you thought of any way of getting there, my pet?"

"Well," he replied, "why couldn't we swim ashore in tubs? I used to swim about in the pond in that way when I was staying with my godfather."

"The very thing!" I cried. "Let us see what can be done at once."

Followed by the children, I at once descended towards the hold of the vessel—now filled with water—where several great casks were floating about empty. I drew four of them out upon the floor of the lower deck, at this time not much above the water-level. They were strong wooden casks, hooped with iron, and appeared to me to be well fitted for our purpose. So, aided by Fritz, I set to work to saw them in halves.

When we had thus obtained eight tubs and ranged them along side by side, I sought out a pliable plank long enough to lie under the whole of them and turn up at each end like a keel. This done, we nailed our tubs firmly to the plank and to each other, and then, to finish the matter, we got two other planks, which we nailed along the sides of the tubs and brought to a point at each end, like the prow and stern of a canoe.

Our work finished, we found ourselves in possession of a contrivance which, in a calm sea, I felt sure would enable us to get to land.

But we were now met by another difficulty. Our boat was so heavy that not with all our strength united could we move, much less launch it.

"We want a screw-jack," I said.

Fritz immediately remembered that he had seen one somewhere and set out to find it.

In the meantime I sawed off some rollers, and when Fritz returned with the jack, I hoisted the contrivance up while he put the rollers under; and now we could move our tub-raft to any part of the vessel we pleased.

A few minutes afterwards we had the pleasure of seeing our newly-made boat slide safely down the lower deck into the sea—so swiftly, however, that she would have been far away from us in an instant if I had not previously taken the precaution of securing her to one of the beams of the wreck by a cable.

Remembering, that savages employ a kind of balance-paddle to keep their canoes steady in the water, I determined to make something of the sort myself.

I found two pieces of a splintered yard which exactly served my purpose. I fastened one of them to each end of the boat—screwing them loosely, so that they might be turned in any direction. Then to the end of each of the arms that thus stretched out over the water I attached an empty keg, which, floating upon the waves, would enable the vessel to keep its balance. We then made some more oars, so that we might have at least one each.

When these various labours were ended it was too late to think of putting to sea that day, so we resigned ourselves to the necessity of passing another night upon the wreck.

This determination taken, my wife prepared for us an excellent repast, which comforted and revived us much, for we had scarcely thought, during the day, of taking either a morsel of bread or a drop of wine.

Though feeling in far less danger than on the previous evening, I took the precaution of again fitting the children with their swimming floats before allowing them to retire to rest; and I advised my wife to dress herself in male clothing, which, as I pointed out, would embarrass her less than her own if the worst should happen after all.

She naturally felt a strong repugnance thus to disguise herself, but at length she yielded to my wishes. Leaving me for a few minutes, she soon re-appeared in the jaunty uniform of a midshipman, which she had found in one of the sea-chests, and which became her admirably.

Sleep was not long in overtaking us, for the day had been very laborious.

The night passed without any untoward incident.

CHAPTER 2

Landing, and the First Day on Shore

At day-break we were all astir; for hope, like grief, is no friend to sleep.

As soon as we had offered up our morning prayer together, I said to my children, "We are now going, by the help of God, to attempt our deliverance from this peril. Give the animals on board provisions for several days; for if our endeavour should succeed, as I devoutly trust it may, we can then return and fetch them. After that, gather together everything that may seem likely to be of any use to us when we disembark; and may God speed us in our undertaking."

I decided that our cargo should comprise, first of all, a barrel of powder, some guns and pistols, and a supply of bullets, together with bullet-moulds and lead to renew our stock when these were gone. Each of us was furnished with a game-bag, which, for the present, we filled with provisions. I provided myself with a case of portable soup made up into cakes, a can of biscuits, an iron pot, and some knives, axes, saws, pincers, nails, gimlets, and fishing-lines. I took also a quantity of sail-cloth, with which I proposed to construct a tent to shelter us from the weather.

In fact, we amassed so many things that I was obliged to leave a large quantity of them behind, though I had already exchanged for articles of necessity everything which I had at first thrown into the tubs as ballast.

Just as we were about to embark, the cocks, by their persistent and melancholy crowing, seemed to be bidding us a sad farewell; whereupon my wife suggested that it would be better to take them with us, together with the hens, the ducks, the geese, and the pigeons. I consented.

Upon that she placed a couple of cocks and a dozen hens into one of the tubs, and I covered them over with a rude lattice-work which we made amongst us by interlacing some of the more pliable splinters strewn about the deck of the ship. As to the geese, the ducks, and the pigeons, I simply set them at liberty, feeling confident that instinct alone would take them to land, the former through the water and the latter through the air.

The children were already embarked in the order which I had assigned them, when my wife returned from the interior of the ship carrying a good-sized, well-filled bag, which she threw into the tub occupied by little Francis. I paid no attention to this bag at the time, thinking that the provident mother had only brought it to make a more comfortable seat for the child.

As soon as we were all safely stowed, I cut the cable by which we were moored to the ship, and we began to row for the shore.

In the first tub was my wife; in the second, little Francis. Fritz occupied the third. The two next contained the powder, the arms, the sail-cloth, the tools, the provisions, and the poultry. Jack was in the sixth, Ernest in the seventh. I had taken the last for myself, and there, with a stern-oar in my hands, I steered our strange vessel. Each of us had one of our swimming floats strapped round us for safety in case of accident.

The dogs being very large, I judged it prudent not to embark them, and left them upon the wreck. When, however, they saw us going away they began to whine piteously. Presently they both jumped into the sea, and soon swam up to us. Fearing that the distance to be traversed was too great for their strength, I showed them how to rest themselves by placing their forepaws upon the barrels that we had hung out to balance the boat. The sagacious animals readily comprehended this manoeuvre, and were thus able to follow us without suffering from too much fatigue.

The sea was calm, its motion being of the gentlest, and its surface flecked here and there with light, fleecy foam. The sky was clear, the sun radiant. We all rowed together; the rising tide running inland favoured us. Around us floated chests, casks, and bales—strays from the wrecked vessel.

Fritz and I laid hold of as many of these as came in our way with our oars, and tying them to our tubs, towed them along with us. My wife, with her hand placed upon the head of her youngest child, and her eyes raised to heaven, prayed silently.

Our voyage proceeded prosperously; but the nearer we came to the coast, the more wild and desolate it seemed. A line of bare grey rocks was the only sight it offered to the view.

Presently, however, Fritz, who had keen powers of vision, declared that he could descry trees on shore, and among them the cocoa-tree.

Ernest, naturally dainty in his tastes, was delighted at the idea of eating freshly-gathered cocoa-nuts, which, as he had read, were so much better than those sold in Europe.

Meanwhile a lively discussion was going on among the children concerning the reality of the trees which Fritz was endeavouring to make them see. While I was expressing my regret that I had not thought to bring away the captain's telescope with me, Jack triumphantly drew from his pocket a smaller one which he had found in the cabin of the boatswain's mate.

I was not able to take a survey of the shore. Forgetting the point in dispute, all I looked for was a favourable place for landing, and I fixed upon a creek towards which the pigeons, now far in advance of us, were directing their course as if they were our advance guard.

We plied our oars bravely, and at length reached the land at the mouth of a stream where there was not more than enough water to float our craft, and where the coast between the rocks was very low.

The children leapt lightly to land, with the exception of Francis, who was too young even to get out of his tub, and had to be helped by his mother.

The dogs, which had reached land before us, testified their joy by bounding round us with loud barkings. The ducks and geese, already installed upon the banks of the stream, welcomed us with a chorus of quacking, with which were mingled the hoarse cries of some penguins that sat immovable upon the surrounding rocks, and several flamingoes which flew away frightened at our approach.

When we landed it was necessary to proceed at once with the unloading of our boat. Everything was soon transported to the bank of the river. It was not much, but how rich did we consider ourselves in its possession!

I selected a suitable spot on which to pitch the tent that was to be our shelter. We then took one of the poles which had been used to balance the boat, and drove it firmly into the ground. To the top of it, crosswise, we tied the other, which we fixed in a fissure of the rock. This formed the framework of our tent. Over it we threw our sail-cloth, which we stretched out as far as it would reach on either side, and fastened to the earth with stakes. This done, I had the chests of provisions and other heavy articles brought in and placed round the edges to keep out the wind; while Fritz put some hooks along the edge of one side of the sail-cloth in front, to enable us to hook the two sides together and so shut ourselves in in the night-time.

Then I sent the children out to gather as much moss and dry herbage as they could find, wherewith to make our beds.

While they were thus occupied I got together some stones, and at a little distance from the tent built up a sort of hearth, upon which I placed some armfuls of dry wood that I picked up along the banks of the stream; and in this way I soon had a great fire lighted and crackling merrily.

My wife then put our pot upon my rude grate, and after she had filled it with water I threw in five or six cakes of the portable soup.

"What are you going to stick together, papa?" asked little Francis, who had mistaken the soup-cakes for glue.

His mother smilingly replied that I was going to make some soup.

"Glue-soup?" he asked, shuddering at the thought of it.

"No, no, my pretty," replied his mother; "nice soup made of meat."

"Meat!" he exclaimed, staring with astonishment. "Are you going to the butcher's then, mamma?"

His mother thereupon laughingly set herself to the task of making him understand that the cakes which he had mistaken for glue were in reality made of the juices of meat, extracted by a peculiar process, and that each of them contained as much nourishment as a pound of beef.

"They adopt this plan," she said, "because fresh meat will not keep during long voyages. This supplies the place of it."

Meanwhile Fritz, who had loaded his gun, went up the banks of the streams to look for game, and Ernest took a stroll along the beach. Jack went hunting among the broken rocks in the hope of finding mussels.

I was employing myself in getting the casks and other wreckage out of the water, when I heard Jack crying out lustily. Armed with an axe, I ran to the place whence his voice came, and there saw him up to his knees in the water.

"Papa, papa!" he cried in a tone of mingled triumph and terror, "do make haste, I have caught such an enormous creature!"

"This is well," I said; "bring it along."

"I cannot, papa; it won't let me."

I felt inclined to laugh at the troubles of this conqueror held prisoner by his captive, but I found it was necessary to go to his help; for a huge lobster had seized him by the leg, and poor Jack tried in vain to release himself from the animal's pincers.

I at once jumped into the water, whereupon the lobster let go his hold and tried to escape; but I managed to seize him by the middle of the body and carry him ashore. My precipitate young friend, Jack, burning with anxiety to show his magnificent captive to his mother, laid hold of the creature with both hands; scarcely had he grasped it, however, when it swung its tail swiftly round and struck him so sharp a blow in the face, that he let it fall at once and began to cry. This time I could not refrain, while offering him my consolations, from laughing heartily at his misfortune. I pointed out to him that nothing was more simple than to render his prisoner perfectly harmless; all he had to do was to take hold of the lobster by the middle of the body. This reassured him, and holding the creature as I had suggested, he set out to bear his prize in triumph to his mother.

"Mamma! Francis! Ernest! Fritz! where is Fritz!" he shouted as he approached the tent. "Come and see! A crab! a crab!"

Ernest, after having gravely inspected the animal, advised that it should then and there be thrown into the pot, as it would render the soup more succulent, a matter of prime importance to one of his dainty tastes. My wife did not seem disposed to rely much upon the excellence of the recipe. She decided that the lobster should be cooked separately.

Ernest then told us that he had himself made a discovery.

"I saw," said he, "some shell-fish in the sea, and, but that I should have wetted my feet, I would have brought some along with me."

"Oh, yes," replied Jack with an amusing air of disdain, "I saw some of those things; but what are they? nothing but mussels. I would not eat one if you were to pay me for it. Look at my lobster—that, now, is something like a shell-fish."

"Who knows," returned Ernest, "but that they may be oysters, and not mussels? Judging from the manner in which they attach themselves to the rocks, and from the depth at which they are found, I should say they were oysters."

"I also saw," added Ernest, "a quantity of salt in the crevices of the rocks. I fancy the sun must have dried the sea-water there."

"You appear to me," replied I, "to be a most valiant talker, Ernest. If you saw a quantity of salt, why did you not scrape some of it together and bring a bagful back with you? Go at once and repair this negligence, in order that we may no longer be compelled to eat soup which is insipid for the want of the very ingredient you have been so fortunate as to discover."

Ernest set out on the instant, and soon returned. The salt which he brought, however, was so mixed with sand that I was about to throw it away, when my wife prevented me.

She dissolved the white dust in water, which she passed through a cloth. This left the sand behind, and we seasoned our soup with the liquor.

The soup was at length ready, but Fritz had not yet returned. Besides, with no vessels before us but the pot, we began to ask each other, somewhat sheepishly, how we were going to eat our savoury dish. Should we be driven to sip out of the boiling cauldron in turn, and fish for the biscuits, which had been put into the soup instead of bread, with our fingers? This was impossible.

"If we only had a few cocoa-nuts," said Ernest, "we might use the broken shells for spoons."

"Would not oyster-shells serve our purpose?" asked Ernest.

"The very thing," cried I. "Run and fetch some at once."

Ernest set out again, but was distanced by Jack, who was already up to his knees in the sea before young Indolence had got to the beach.

Jack detached the oysters from the rocks and threw them upon the sands, while Ernest picked them up, being still very careful not to wet his feet.

At the same time that our oyster-fishers returned, Fritz put in an appearance. He advanced slowly, with one hand behind his back, and put on a hopeless kind of look, as if praying our pity.

"What, have you found nothing?" I asked.

"Nothing at all," he replied.

But his brothers, who surrounded him, suddenly began crying out, "Oh, a guinea-pig! Where did you find it, Fritz? Let me look at it!"

Upon this, Fritz proudly drew forth the game which he had at first so carefully concealed.

I congratulated him upon the success of his sport, but I did not fail at the same time to reprimand him for the falsehood which he had permitted himself to tell, though it was only done in fun, and intended not to deceive but to surprise us.

He begged me to pardon him his error, and then he proceeded to tell us how he had crossed to the other side of the stream, and had there found that the country was entirely different to that which was on the side where we were.

"Down there," he said, "the vegetation is magnificent. Moreover, there are upon the shore a quantity of chests and casks, and other waifs from the wreck which the sea has cast up. Shall we permit all these things to rot there? Shall we not go as soon as possible to fetch the beasts off the vessel? The cow especially will give us excellent milk to soak our biscuit in, and down below there, there is splendid herbage for her to feed upon; to say nothing of the noble trees that will afford shelter for ourselves. Let us make our home there. Quit this barren and cheerless spot, and——"

"Patience! patience, Fritz!" I replied. "One thing at a time. Tomorrow will follow today, and each day has its appointed duties. But before all, tell me—did you discover any trace of our hapless fellow-travellers?"

"Nothing—neither upon land nor at sea. Nor have I seen any living thing except a troop of animals similar to that which I have brought with me. They are, I think, guinea-pigs, but of a peculiar species, for their feet are formed like those of hares. They are not at all timid, so that I was able to observe them very closely. They leap about among the herbage, and seating themselves on their hinder legs, carry their food to their mouths like squirrels."

Ernest, putting on his most learned look, examined the animal very carefully, and finally pronounced that, according to his reading of natural history, he believed himself authorised to declare the supposed guinea-pig to be an agouti.

Jack was exerting himself to the utmost to open an oyster with a knife; but, although he put forth all his strength, and twisted his face into the oddest contortions, he could not succeed.

I relieved him of his difficulty. I took some oysters and placed them upon the hot embers. Here they very soon opened themselves.

"There, my children," said I, "behold the food that gourmands most prize! Taste it."

With these words, I took out an oyster and swallowed it.

Jack and Fritz followed my example, but they at once declared that the delicacy was detestable. Ernest and Francis confirmed this judgment.

So we only made use of that part of the oyster which is ordinarily thrown away, and threw away that part of it which is ordinarily eaten. Employing the shells as spoons, we began to eat our soup.

As we finished our repast the sun was sinking below the horizon, and the fowls and the ducks came clamouring around us for food.

It was now that I discovered the use to which my good wife had put the sack which she had thrown into one of the tubs of our boat, as I thought, for little Francis to sit upon. She brought it out from the tent, and thrusting her hand into it, scattered abroad a quantity of grain, upon which our feathered friends pounced hungrily.

I praised her highly for her foresight, but I also remarked that it would be much better to save the grain for seed than to waste it upon animals which could be fed well enough on damaged biscuit.

Having partaken of their evening meal, the pigeons flew off to the ledges of the rocks, and the fowls perched themselves upon the ridge of the tent, and the ducks waddled away to take refuge in some beds of rushes at the mouth of the stream which ran into the bay.

We, in our turn, prepared for repose. The arms were charged and so placed that we could lay hold upon them at first alarm of danger, and we offered up our evening prayer and retired into the tent.

The suddenness with which the darkness succeeded the daylight greatly astonished the children. For my own part I concluded therefrom that we were in a region near the equator, or at all events in some part of the tropics.

I took one more look outside the tent to assure myself that all was peaceful around us, and then closing the entrance, retired to rest. The night was very chilly; we were obliged to lie as close together as possible to preserve our natural warmth. This contrast between the heat of the day and the coldness of the night confirmed me in the opinion I had formed concerning the geographical position of the region in which we found ourselves.

My wife slept. So did the children. It was agreed between us that I should keep watch half the night, and then awake my wife to take my place. But sweetly and insensibly slumber fell upon me; and God alone kept guard over us during the first night that we passed in the land of our deliverance.

CHAPTER 3

An Exploring Expedition

The cocks were the first to salute the rising sun, and my wife and I were awakened by their song. We at once took counsel together upon the occupations of the day and determined that I and Fritz should set out upon an exploring expedition, while my wife remained in the neighbourhood of the tent with the other children.

We hastened our steps, and very soon the murmuring of the stream whose course we were following drowned the distant farewells of our loved ones. In order to cross the stream, it was necessary to travel to a place where it leapt over the steep rocks in the form of a cascade. At the top of the fall the water was narrower and more shallow, and by stepping upon pieces of broken rock we were enabled to cross safely.

Upon the opposite bank Nature changed her aspect entirely. We found ourselves at first in the midst of an expanse of tall grass, dried by the sun and very tough, through which we made our way slowly and with difficulty.

After we had gone about two leagues we entered a wood. At every step some magnificent shrub or strange tree offered itself to our view.

Fritz, who marvelled at every new sight, suddenly cried out, "Oh, papa! What are these trees with large swellings on their trunks?"

I recognised the calabash, the flexible trunk of which winds itself round larger trees, and holds drooping from its stem the gourd with its hard, dry shell. This shell, I told Fritz, was often used for dishes, basins, bottles and spoons.

We had each taken a calabash, which we were trying to turn into some vessel or other for use in the household. Fritz endeavoured to cut his with his knife, and not being successful, flung it away. I wound a piece of string round the gourd, and drawing it tighter and tighter, I succeeded in breaking the shell neatly in two, and found myself possessed of a couple of basins of equal size.

"Well," said Fritz, "that would never have occurred to me. How did you think of it?"

"The merit of the invention," I replied, "is not mine. I only remember to have read somewhere that the device is employed by savage tribes who have no knives, and I thought that I would put it into practice."

Having witnessed my own success in basin-making, Fritz took courage and set to work again—this time with string instead of a knife.

Between us we made as many vessels as we thought would be useful. These I laid out in the sun to dry, having previously filled them with sand to prevent them from being drawn out of shape. Then, in order that we might find them on our return, we carefully noted the spot where we had placed them.

We pursued our journey, employing ourselves as we went in cutting spoons out of the fragments of two or three calabashes which we had broken while making our basins. Rough as they were, our gourd-spoons were marvels of convenience compared with the oyster-shells with which we had been obliged to eat our soup on the previous evening.

After having walked steadily on for about three hours, we came to a tongue of land which ran far out into the sea, and ended in a lofty hill, up which we climbed with some difficulty. At our feet glittered the sea in an immense bay, the shores of which were clothed with many-coloured foliage, that stretched away on either hand to a dimly-seen cape. The sun darted down his most ardent beams at the time, and I told Fritz to follow me to the grateful shadow of a grove of palm-trees which I saw in the distance.

He was walking before. I told him to cut himself a reed as a weapon against serpents.

He did as he was told, and it was not long before I heard him crying out in transports of joy, "Sugar-cane! What exquisite juice! How delighted my mother and my brothers will be! I will take home a bundle of these canes for my mother and the boys. They will be delighted to feast upon them; and besides that, we can use one or two to refresh ourselves upon the road." He cut nearly a dozen of the very largest he could find, stripped them of their leaves, and tucked them under his arm.

Hardly had we got into the palm-grove when a troop of monkeys, alarmed by our approach, sprang into the trees, from the topmost branches of which they looked down upon us in terror, uttering piercing cries and grimacing horribly. I flung some stones up towards the monkeys, without any intention of striking them. At once, obeying their natural instinct for imitation, they began to pick from the tops of the palms a quantity of cocoa-nuts, which they flung down upon us in wild emulation. It was not difficult to avoid these missiles, for they were by no means well aimed.

As soon as the shower of nuts slackened, Fritz gathered up as many as he could carry, and we moved out of reach of the monkeys.

First of all we opened the small apertures near the stalk of the fruit with the points of our knives, and thence drank the milk which the shell contained. To our great surprise, however, we did not find this liquor to be so good as we had thought it would be. The cream which adhered to the inside of the shell seemed to us to be better. So we broke open the nuts with our axes, scraped the cream into our calabash spoons, sweetened it with sugar out of our canes, and made a delicious meal.

We felt very much refreshed by it, and trudged along more lightly than ever.

Before long we came again to the place where we had left our gourd vessels. They were perfectly dry now, and we took them up to carry back with us.

A little farther on, Turk dashed barking amongst a troop of monkeys, who were gambolling peacefully on the ground. At the first barkings the creatures dispersed themselves. In a moment, indeed, they had all disappeared with the exception of a she-monkey who was giving suck to her little one, and who was seized upon by Turk and worried.

Fritz at once rushed off to save her, but when he reached the spot the poor beast was dead, and the dog had already begun to devour her.

The little monkey leapt upon Fritz's shoulder and clung there tightly.

"Oh, papa," Fritz cried, "let me keep it! It will die if we abandon it."

"So be it, then, my boy," I replied.

While we were discoursing thus, the imperturbable Turk tranquilly finished his odious repast.

"Friend Turk," said Fritz, with solemnity, pointing the while at the monkey, which he had now taken on his arm, "you have made an orphan; you have eaten the mother of this poor innocent. It is only just that you should replace her."

Then passing a cord round Turk's neck, he gave the end of it to the monkey, which he seated upon the astonished dog's back, after the manner of a horseman. Turk accepted his new duty with a very ill grace at first, but after a sharp reprimand he submitted; and the droll little animal, completely reassured, appeared to find the place in which Fritz had installed him convenient and comfortable.

At length we found ourselves in the midst of the family, who were awaiting us on the bank of the stream.

The dogs saluted one another afar off by loud barkings; and Turk's part in the greeting so frightened the little monkey that he again leapt upon Fritz's shoulder, and could not be persuaded to come off.

Scarcely had the children caught sight of us, when they burst into loud shouts of joy; and when, as we came closer, they saw the monkey crouching tremblingly upon Fritz's shoulder, their delight knew no bounds.

At once we were surrounded by little hands which were busy to relieve us of our loads.

On reaching the tent we found that our good friends who had come to meet us had made every preparation for giving us a substantial repast.

Our pot full of appetising soup stood bubbling on the top of the fire, and while fish were being grilled on one side of it, a large goose was roasting on the other—the shell of yesterday's lobster being placed beneath it to catch the fat. Hard by stood a staved-in cask filled with excellent Dutch cheese; so that we had a variety of eatables before us, all calculated to excite our appetites—which, I may remark, had been rather coquetted with than satisfied by what we had eaten during the day.

At the same time, I could not help remarking to my wife that I thought she had begun to kill our poultry very soon, and that in my opinion, much as I should enjoy the dish when it was served up, it would have been far better to leave the creature alive in order that it might multiply its species for the future.

"Make yourself quite easy, love, on that point," said my wife; "our stock of provisions will be but very slightly diminished by the meal before us. Little Francis caught the fish. I myself found the cask of cheese on the beach, and the fowl was brought down by Ernest, who gives it a very strange name."

"I gave it the right name," interrupted our young scholar; "I called it a stupid penguin. As to its being stupid there can be no doubt whatever, for it allowed me to come close up to it and kill it with a stick. That it is a penguin I know, for it has all the peculiarities of that bird mentioned in the natural histories. It has four claws, which are united by a web, and it has short legs. It sits in one position for hours together, and, as it sits, looks in shape something like a bottle. Moreover, its beak is long and strong, and curved over at the end."

I congratulated the young savant upon the good use he had made of his reading, and then we sat ourselves in a circle on the sand to commence our repast. Each of us was furnished with a calabash basin and spoon.

The children, while waiting for the soup to cool, broke some of the cocoa-nuts and eagerly drank the milk, which, as I have said before, was none of the best. Then we attacked the soup, and after that the fish, which I cannot but confess was a little too dry. Next we fell-to upon the penguin, which had a strong flavour as of train-oil about it. This, however, did not prevent us from enjoying so sumptuous a repast; for a good appetite always makes a good dinner.

The monkey, as was natural, became an object of general attention. The children dipped the corners of their handkerchiefs into the cocoa-nut milk and gave them him to suck, thinking that by this device he would not miss his mother so much. The little creature took to his food so intelligently, and with so excellent an appetite, that we had no longer any fear of not being able to rear him. We decided that we would call him Nip.

Fritz asked me whether I did not think that with so capital a dinner before us we might venture to indulge in some of his cocoa-champagne.

"Taste it first," replied I, "and see if you can conscientiously offer it to us to drink."

Scarcely had he placed the bottle to his lips when he took it away again, and with a ludicrous grimace cried out, "Pah! why, it's vinegar!"

"I told you that was how it would be," I said. "But no matter. Out of evil comes good. This vinegar will do admirably to eat with our fish: it will take off the dryness which we perceived in them."

Thereupon I poured a little of the liquid into my gourd-plate, and all the rest following my example, we soon made an end of the fish that we had previously left. Finally we took some cheese, and also used our vinegar with that.

The repast finished, and the sun fast sinking below the horizon, we offered up our evening prayer, and retired to our mossy beds in the tent.

Fritz and Jack placed Nip between them, and covered him well to keep him warm. "He is our child," they said laughingly.

As was the case on the previous night, I took another look outside the tent after slumber had fallen upon my family, and finding everything peaceful, closed the door, retired to my bed, and was soon sound asleep with my dear ones around me.

I could not have been asleep long, however, when I was awakened by the yelping of the dogs and the fluttering of the fowls, which were perched upon the top of the tent.

I leapt up at once, and went outside, followed by my wife and Fritz, who did not sleep so soundly as his brothers. We each of us had taken the precaution of carrying a weapon with us.

By the clear light of the moon, we saw our dogs engaged in a fierce struggle with a half-score of jackals.

Our brave guardians had already laid three of them by the heels, but seemed in danger of being compelled to give in to numbers had we not come to their succour. Fritz and I fired together. Two of our nocturnal visitors fell dead at once; the remainder, frightened by the reports of the guns, scampered away as fast as their legs could carry them.

Fritz desired to carry the animal which he had killed into the tent with him, in order to show it to his brothers in the morning, and I gave him permission to do so. We left the other four to the dogs.

We then returned to the side of our little sleepers, whom neither the barking of the dogs nor the firing of the guns had awakened.

Very soon we were all wrapped in slumber again, and nothing further occurred to disturb us during the remainder of the night.

CHAPTER 4

A Voyage to the Wreck

At the first break of dawn I awoke my wife, in order to consult with her again as to the employments of the day.

"My beloved," I said, "I see so many urgent duties before us that I know not to which to give the priority. On the one hand it is clear that if we desire to save the cattle on the wreck, and to recover the various articles there that will be of use to us, it will be necessary to make a voyage thither at once. On the other hand, I cannot fail to see that it is almost equally necessary to set about building a more comfortable dwelling-place for at any moment a storm may overtake us in these tropical regions, and then the effect of it will be as disastrous to us on land as it will be at sea. I confess that I do not know which we ought to do first—recover all we can from the wreck, or make our habitation secure where we are."

"Pray do not weary yourself," she replied, "by forecasting events. What remains on the wreck is perishable. As to our dwelling, a day or two will make no great change in our prospects."

"It is well," I said. "I shall set out for the wreck with Fritz, leaving you and the other children to do what you can on land while we are away."

"Come, come!" I cried, "jump up, jump up! The sun has already risen, and we have no time to lose."

Fritz was the first to put in an appearance, and, profiting by the time spent by his brothers in rubbing their eyes and shaking off their drowsiness, he placed his dead jackal in front of the tent in order to witness the surprise which it would cause them.

He had reckoned without the dogs, who, seeing one of their nocturnal combatants yet remaining, and believing it to be still living, flung themselves upon it, barking furiously.

Fritz had the greatest difficulty in driving them away.

The yelping of the animals, and Fritz's wild shouting at them, brought the young idlers out all the more speedily.

They made their appearance one by one, the little monkey perching upon the shoulder of Jack. No sooner did he set eyes upon the jackal, however, than he became so frightened that he flew back into the tent, and buried himself so deeply in the moss of our beds that nothing could be seen of him but his tiny nozzle.

As Fritz had expected, his brothers were greatly astonished at the sight of the jackal.

Then we took breakfast; for the youngsters were of that class whose appetites awaken with their eyes.

A case of biscuits was opened, and the barrel of cheese again laid under contribution.

All at once, Ernest, who had been prowling about among the barrels which we had fished out of the sea, cried out, "Oh! papa, would not our biscuit be much nicer if we were to eat it with butter?"

"There you are again with your eternal 'if'," I replied. "You are always awakening our desires without giving us the means of satisfying them. Are you content with cheese?"

"I did not say I was not," he answered; "but if some one would break open this barrel——"

"What barrel?" I said.

"This one," he replied. "I feel certain that it contains butter, for there oozes from the joints of it a kind of fatty matter which has exactly the same smell."

After having satisfied ourselves that Ernest's nose had not deceived him, we consulted gravely as to the best plan of getting enough butter for our present supply without risking the loss of the remainder.

Fritz was for removing the hoops, and taking out the head of the cask.

I thought that if this were done it would loosen the staves, and let the butter run away when it became melted by the sun. It seemed to me to be wiser to make a hole in the side with a chisel, and extract thence with a piece of stick as much butter as we wanted.

This plan being adopted, we soon had some excellent toast, the taste of which rendered us doubly desirous of saving the cow from the wreck.

The dogs, fatigued by their nocturnal combat, slept tranquilly at our feet. I remarked that they had not come out of their fight with the jackals scatheless, and particularly pointed to some ugly wounds upon their necks.

Thereupon my wife hit upon the happy device of washing the butter till she had got all the salt out of it, and anointing their wounds with what remained. The dogs patiently submitted to this dressing of their sores, and afterwards began to lick each other —a proceeding which gave me hope that they would soon be cured.

"It is important," said Fritz, "that they should be furnished for similar occasions with spiked collars."

"Yes," said Jack, "and if mamma will help me I will undertake to make them some during the day."

"With all my heart," said his mother; "I will do everything I can to help you, and we shall see how you succeed."

"Yes, my boy," I added in my turn, "use all your ingenuity, and if you can hit upon a practicable plan of carrying out your design, we will do our best to carry it into execution."

"As to you, Fritz," I continued, "prepare yourself to accompany me on a voyage which I propose making to the wreck. Your mother and I have decided this morning that we shall do so; and, as was the case yesterday, she will remain here with the other children while we go to endeavour to save the cattle, and whatever else is likely to be of use to us."

Our tub-boat was soon got ready. As we were setting out, we arranged with my wife that she should set up on the shore a pole with a piece of white rag tied to it, as a sort of signal to us when we were upon the wreck. In case of distress she was to pull it down and to fire a gun three times in succession. I then induced her—so courageous had she become—to consent to our remaining on board the wreck for a night, in case we should not be able to get everything ready for an earlier departure. In that case we agreed to burn lights to show that all was well.

Knowing that there were provisions still left in the vessel, we took only our arms. I permitted Fritz to take his monkey, to whom he promised a rare feast of goat's-milk.

Fritz rowed vigorously, and I did my best to assist him while steering the craft with an oar thrust out from the stern.

When we had got some distance, I noticed that a river, much larger and more rapid than that upon which we had pitched our tent, emptied itself into the bay; and I conjectured that in doing so it would form a current which, if we once got into it, would help us on our journey. We pulled in the direction of this current, which, as I had anticipated, carried us, without any further effort of our own, over more than three parts of our voyage. A few stout pulls with our oars brought us to our destination.

We boarded the vessel and moored our boat securely to its side. Fritz's first thought was to run to the animals, which, as soon as they heard us aboard, began lowing and bleating piteously. The poor creatures displayed the liveliest satisfaction at seeing us again, and ate up the fresh provender and water that we gave them with avidity. Having fed our dumb companions, we next made an excellent repast ourselves: we had no difficulty in procuring it, for the ship had been provisioned for a long voyage.

The ingenious Fritz then tried an experiment which succeeded to admiration. He introduced his monkey to the goat, who thereupon gave him such as if he had been her own offspring. It is needless to say that Nip made a hearty and delicious meal.

"Now, Fritz," said I, "what will it be best to do first?"

"I think," he said, "that before proceeding further we ought to set up a sail in our boat."

It did not seem to me on the first blush of the thing that this was a very urgent matter; but Fritz pointed out to me that, during our voyage across, he had noticed a strong head wind, against which we should have had to struggle stoutly, had it not been for the river current; and he said he thought he knew enough about sailing to be able to utilise this wind on the return voyage. He also mentioned that he thought we should have a good deal of difficulty in getting back, in any case, with all our tubs loaded and only two oarsmen, one of whom was partly engaged in steering.

This reasoning appeared to me to be so sensible that I gave in to it at once.

I sought out a piece of broken yard large enough to serve as a mast, and a slighter piece to which to fix our sail. Fritz meanwhile nailed a thick plank across one of the tubs and bored a large hole in it. Through this hole we thrust our mast, and then attached pulleys to our sail in such a manner that I could easily manoeuvre it and steer the boat at the same time.

To finish with, Fritz—who, as was natural at his age, was given to mingle amusement and work together—tied to the top of the mast a long pennon of red bunting, and watched it float out in the wind with childish delight.

While smiling at his innocent diversion, I directed towards the bay whence we set out the large telescope which I had formerly seen on the captain's table, but had forgotten to carry away with me. I saw with joy that my wife and my little ones were peacefully engaged in various occupations, without a suspicion that I was a silent observer of all they were doing.

It was now growing late, and it became clear that it would be of no use to attempt to reach land again that night. So we spent the remainder of the day in pillaging the wrecked vessel, as if we had been pirates, and in filling our tubs with whatever was likely to prove of use to us.

In anticipation of a lengthy sojourn in the uninhabited country in which we had taken our refuge, I gave the preference to tools which would aid us in our labours to sustain life, and to arms which would protect us if attacked.

The vessel, as it so happened, was an emigrant ship, whose destination was the Southern Seas—among the islands of which we and our fellow-passengers had intended to settle as colonists. She was therefore well stocked with provisions and utensils of a kind which would not have been found had she been bound upon an ordinary voyage; so we had free choice among a multitude of objects suitable for the isolated life that loomed before us in the future.

I selected a large assortment of saucepans, plates, dishes, basins, knives, forks, and other domestic utensils, while Fritz took possession of a service of plate which he found in the captain's cabin, and some bottles of wine and spirits, to which I added a few Westphalia hams. These luxuriant provisions, however, did not lead us to contemn certain sacks of wheat and maize and other grain. Also I took possession of a compass, and some spades and other garden implements, together with a further supply of guns, pistols, and ammunition. Furthermore, we supplied ourselves with hammocks, bedclothes, cord and twine of all kinds, and sail-cloth; and even took care to place among our cargo a little keg of sulphur with which to renew our supply of matches when those we had were all used in lighting our daily fire.

I then declared our cargo complete; when Fritz arrived with a last package.

"Leave that," I said, "my dear boy. We have no room for anything so large and apparently so heavy as what you have there."

"Oh! do let us take it," he said; "it is the captain's library, containing books of science and natural history, together with accounts of travels, and a Bible. Ernest and my mother will be so pleased with them!"

"My dear boy," I replied, "you are very thoughtful. Food for the mind is as essential as food for the body, and I heartily consent to do as you desire. Your last discovery will be a treasure to all of us."

Our boat was now so heavily laden that it sunk almost to the water's edge, and had not the sea been perfectly calm I should have lightened it. As it was, I merely took the precaution to preserve our swimming floats, in case it should founder in the night and leave us helpless.

Night fell suddenly. A large fire which we perceived upon the distant coast assured us that nothing untoward had overtaken our beloved ones on land. And by way of reply to this good news, I hung out three lighted lanterns upon the side of the wreck. Immediately the report of a gun gave us notice that our signal had been seen.

Our preparations were soon made to pass the night in our tub-boat. I did not think it safe to sleep on board the wreck, for it was so placed that the least gust of wind might overturn it, and in that case we should be in serious danger of not seeing land again.

In spite of the discomfort of his berth, Fritz was not long in falling sound asleep. As for me, I could not close my eyes for an instant. I was full of anxiety for the safety of those whom we had left on shore, and, at the same time, desirous of being ready for any emergency that might arise where we were.

No sooner did day begin to break, than I mounted the deck of the vessel and directed my telescope towards the shore. I saw my wife come out of the tent and look anxiously towards us. I immediately ran a strip of white cloth up the mast, and my wife thereupon lowered and raised her flag three times, to show that she had understood my signal.

"Heaven be praised!" I ejaculated, "they are all safe and well. Now let us see what can be done to get the cattle to land."

"Supposing we were to construct a raft?" said Fritz.

I pointed out to him, not only the difficulty of making such a contrivance, but the far greater difficulty—if not impossibility—of steering it when it was made.

"Very well, then," he replied, "let us push them into the sea. I should think they would be able to swim to land. The pig, at all events, with its fat sides, can be in no possible danger of drowning."

"Perhaps not," I said, "but what about the donkey, the cow, the goat, and the sheep; will they accomplish the journey so easily? For I must tell you candidly that I would willingly sacrifice the pig, if we could thereby save the other animals."

"I have got it, papa!" cried Fritz joyously. "Let us furnish them with the swimming floats which we made for ourselves. It will be splendid to see animals swimming in attire of that kind!"

"Bravo, my noble Fritz!" I exclaimed; "your idea, however droll it may be, seems to be quite practicable. To work, boy! to work! Let us make the attempt at all events."

Thereupon we took a sheep, and having fastened the floats to it, one on each side, pushed it into the sea.

At first the poor beast, frightened out of its wits, disappeared beneath the waves. But it soon rose struggling to the surface; and at length, feeling the support which it derived from the swimming-belt, it floated patient and immovable. We had no longer any doubt that it could swim excellently.

Thus satisfied that we had hit upon the right plan of saving our cattle, we set to work vigorously.

Every piece of cork we could find anywhere was laid under contribution for the smaller animals; and for the larger ones—the cow and the donkey—we prepared empty barrels, which we tied to their sides with cords and strips of cloth.

When all our animals were harnessed, I tied to the horns or the neck of each of them a strong cord to lead them by when we got aboard our boat.

This done, we got them all into the water without much difficulty. The ass alone, after the manner of his kind, was recalcitrant, so we pushed him in backwards. At first he struggled a good deal, but after a time he resigned himself to the necessities of the case, and began to swim with so good a grace that we could not refrain from applauding his superior skill.

As soon as we had entered our boat I unmoored her, and the breeze filling our sail, we found ourselves drifting rapidly and easily landwards.

Fritz, supremely happy in the result of his expedition, alternately fondled his monkey, and looked proudly up to the red streamer which unfurled itself gaily to the wind. For my own part, I followed with eye and heart the movements of my well-beloved ones on land, who, I saw by the aid of my telescope, were hastening down to the beach to meet us.

All at once Fritz cried out, "Father! father! There is an enormous fish coming towards us!"

"To arms!" I said, "and attention!"

Our guns were already charged and we stood ready to fire. The creature of which Fritz had just signalled the approach was neither more nor less than a shark of the very largest kind.

"Let us fire together," said I, "at the moment when the monster, who swims on the surface, opens his jaws to seize that sheep towards which he is making so swiftly."

Our guns went off together, and the shark disappeared.

An instant afterwards we saw, shining upon the surface, the brilliant scales of his belly; and a long trail of blood showed us that we were rid for ever of the terrible corsair.

I ordered Fritz to re-charge his gun, and did the same myself, lest the shark, as its custom is, should not be alone. Happily my fears were ill-founded.

Without meeting with any further adventure, we at length reached the shore.

My wife and the three boys awaited us. They seized the cable that I threw them to make fast the boat. The animals, who came to land without assistance, were soon relieved of their floats. The donkey capered about the sand joyously, and translated the pleasure he felt at once more touching the solid earth into a prolonged and not over-musical "he-haw!"

As soon as we had embraced, and congratulated each other upon meeting again in health and safety after so long and perilous a separation, we went and seated ourselves upon the grass by the side of the stream, where I gave an account of all that had befallen us during our absence. I did not refrain from giving Fritz the high praise he merited for the assistance he had rendered me in our difficult and dangerous task.

CHAPTER 5

What Passed on Land during our Absence

Fritz's invention for transporting the cattle excited general admiration, though little Francis marvelled most at seeing the sail and the bright red pennon.

We were then required to recount, down to the smallest details, how we had conducted our expedition.

Curiosity satisfied on this point, we proceeded to unload our tubs.

Jack soon gave up this drudgery, and went off among the cattle, where, jumping upon the back of the donkey, which had not yet been disembarrassed of its barrels, he rode back towards us with a ludicrous air of mock-majesty. We had all the trouble in the world to remain serious in the face of so droll a spectacle. But what was our astonishment to see our young cavalier wearing a hairy belt, into which he had thrust a pair of pistols!

"Where did you pick up that brigand's costume?" asked I.

"It is all of our own making," he replied, "and so are those," pointing to the necks of the two dogs, each of which was furnished with a leather collar bristling with the spikes of nails. "I think they will be able to defend themselves now," he added, with an air of supreme satisfaction.

"Bravo, my son!" I cried; "but are these your own inventions?"

"Mamma helped me," he replied, "in all the sewing that had to be done."

"But where did you get the leather, the needles, and the thread?" I asked of my wife.

"Fritz's jackal furnished us with the leather," said Jack.

"And as to the rest," added my wife, smiling, "a woman of management is always well provided with needles and thread."

I saw that Fritz was not very well satisfied that his jackal should have been thus appropriated without his permission. It is true he concealed his ill-humour as well as he was able, but on coming near

Jack he held his nose, and cried out, "Pah! what an abominable smell!"

"Yes," replied Jack imperturbably, "it is my belt. It will be all right when it gets dry."

"Let Jack remain to the windward," said I, sailor fashion, "and then he will not annoy us."

"Ah, ah!" said the children, laughing, "to the windward, Jack! to the windward!"

As to the merry Jack himself, he was not in the least troubled by the odour of his belt, but strutted about, handling his pistols like a buccaneer.

His brothers hastened to throw the offensive remains of the jackal into the sea.

Seeing that it was nearly supper-time, I told Fritz to go and fetch one of the Westphalia hams out of the tubs.

He was not long in returning.

"Oh, a ham! a ham ready to eat!" cried the youngsters, clapping their hands.

"Moderate yourselves, my children," said my wife, "for if you only had this ham, which is not yet cooked, for supper, you would fast a long time, I am thinking. But I have here some turtles' eggs, with which I will make an omelette in the frying-pan which papa and Fritz have been thoughtful enough to bring away from the wreck—a nice, savoury omelette, in which butter shall not be wanting."

"The eggs of the turtle," said Ernest, always desirous of displaying his knowledge, "are easily distinguished by their roundness, by their membraneous shells, which are like wetted parchment, and also by the fact that the turtle alone deposits its eggs in the sands by the seashore."

"How did you find them?" asked I.

"That," said my wife, "belongs to a little history which we have to tell you. But before beginning it, I think it will be best to see to the cooking, unless you would like to go to bed supperless."

"You are right," I said; "make an omelette, and reserve your story for the repast. It will form an agreeable side-dish. In the meantime I and the children will stow our cargo in a safe place, and rack up the beasts for the night."

With these words I got up, and the boys followed me to the beach. By the time my wife invited us to do honour to her supper we had finished.

Nothing was wanting to a good meal—omelette, cheese, biscuit, all were found excellent; and a table for the first time decently laid out added not a little to the agreeableness of the repast.

Francis alone, faithful to his calabash service, declined even to return to silver-plate.

"It is far nicer," he said, "to eat out of playthings than out of real dishes."

The dogs, the chickens, the goats, and the sheep formed a circle of interested spectators around us. As to the ducks and geese, I did not trouble myself about feeding them, knowing that the marshy ground at the mouth of the stream would furnish them with abundance of worms and small crabs—to which latter they had already shown themselves partial.

Supper ended, I told Fritz to bring us a bottle of the excellent wine which he had found in the captain's cabin, and begged my wife to take a glass to fortify her for her narrative.

"It seems, then," she said laughingly, "that it has at last come to my turn to recount my noble deeds. As to the first day, I have nothing to tell—anxiety for your safety kept me upon the beach all day, and I had not the courage to undertake a single duty away from thence. I was not a little thankful, I can assure you, when I saw that you reached the wreck without impediment.

"We passed the day, then, in the neighbourhood of the tent; and I confined myself to thinking out a project whereby, on the morrow, we might seek out some spot more comfortable for a dwelling-place than this inhospitable shore. We are here exposed to the full heat of the sun by day, and the full rigour of the cold by night. I thought of the wood you and Fritz had passed through on the previous day, and determined to go thither and explore it.

"This morning, while I was again thinking over my project—without having said anything to the children, who had but just got up—Jack took Fritz's jackal, and cut out from the skin of the animal two large strips, which he deprived of the hair and cleaned as well as he was able.

"He then obtained some long nails, which he drove through one of the strips, and cut out a piece of sail-cloth with which to line it. This done, he brought his work to me, and asked me to sew the cloth to the leather in such a manner that it would at once keep to the nails and cover them. In spite of the disagreeable odour of the skin I did as he desired, and, cutting the strap in two, he put one-half round each of the dogs' necks, as you see. He then desired me to line the other strap, in order that he might wear it as a belt; but I pointed out to him that as this strap was not dry yet, it would shrink and render our labour useless.

"Ernest laughingly advised him to stretch the strap on a board, and carry it about in the sun to dry, which he proceeded very gravely to do, without perceiving the joke.

"I then communicated to the boys my plans for the day, and they fell in with them joyfully. In a twinkling they were furnished forth with arms and provisions. I took a can of water and an axe. Escorted by the dogs, we set out for the banks of the stream.

"Turk, who remembered well enough the way he had travelled with you, was evidently impressed with the responsibilities of his position. He preceded us with an air of superior knowledge, and was continually looking behind to assure himself that we were following in the right track.

"Ernest and Jack marched resolutely behind Turk, proud of carrying arms for the first time in their lives. They also were impressed with their importance, for I had hinted to them that upon their courage and address depended the security of the whole party. And I cannot but confess that, in the circumstances in which we found ourselves, I appreciated, for the first time, your wisdom in teaching them the use of arms, and the necessity for confronting every kind of danger bravely.

"We found it by no means an easy task to cross the stream, the stepping-stones were so wet and slippery. Ernest crossed first without accident. Jack held my bottle and axe, and I took Francis upon my back. The little fellow clasped his arms round my neck and clung to me with all his strength; and with some difficulty and danger we at length got safely over.

"On reaching the other side, and ascending the height whence you saw the splendid prospect that you described to us with so much enthusiasm, my heart, for the first time since our ship-wreck, gave way to the influence of pleasure and hope.

"We soon descended into a dale overshadowed with foliage and carpeted with greensward.

"A small wood lay in front of us; but in order to get there, we had to pass through a large field of grass, so tall and entangled that it both concealed the children and impeded our movements. Jack, however, found a place where the grass was trodden down, and we concluded that we were then in the track which you had made and followed on the previous day. Guided by your footsteps, we, after several times losing one or two of the children in the grass, came out at the entrance to the wood.

"All at once we heard a great rustling among the leaves, and immediately saw a huge bird rise off the ground in front of us, and fly swiftly skywards.

"Each of my little men brought his gun to his shoulder, but the bird was beyond reach before they could take aim at him.

" 'What a pity,' said Ernest rather irritably, 'that I had not got my own little gun with me! Even as it was I should have brought down my bird if he had not flown away so swiftly.'

" 'No doubt,' I replied, 'you would be an excellent sportsman if the game were to give you a quarter of an hour's notice of its intention to fly away.'

" 'But how was I to tell that a bird was going to rise in front of me?' he asked.

" 'It is,' I replied, 'just such surprises as these that make shooting difficult. In order to succeed in sport, it is not only necessary to be a good marksman, but you must also possess great presence of mind.'

" 'What could this bird have been?' asked Jack.

" 'An eagle, of course,' replied Francis. 'It had immensely large wings.'

" 'That proves nothing,' said Ernest; 'all birds with large wings are not eagles.'

" 'I have no doubt,' I interposed, 'that it was sitting upon its nest when we disturbed it. Let us look about, and if we find this nest, we shall then be better able to tell what the bird was.'

"Jack, the madcap, dashed instantly towards the place where the bird had risen, and another bird, exactly like the first, flew out and away, striking the little fellow in the face with its huge wing as it went.

"Jack stood wonder-stricken, and, I think, very much terrified.

"Ernest, not less astonished, made no attempt even to raise his gun towards the bird.

" 'You are pretty sportsmen, truly,' said I. 'Is it possible that you could profit so little by what I have been saying to you? It is clear that you badly need some more lessons in shooting from your father.'

"Ernest was annoyed.

"Jack took off his hat, and, making a comic salute to the fugitive—who by this time was but a dot in the blue sky—'Farewell for the present, Mr. Bird,' said he; 'another time will do as well for me. I am your humble and devoted servant always.'

"Ernest soon found the nest we were looking for. It was very rudely constructed, and contained nothing but a few broken eggshells; from which latter circumstances we concluded that a nest of young ones had not long since occupied it.

"'These birds cannot be eagles,' said Ernest, 'for the young of eagles cannot run so soon after they are born as these birds seem to have done. The contrary is the case with ordinary farmyard hens, guinea-fowl, and other winged creatures of the same family. I am led to assume, then, that the birds whose nest we have just found are bustards; for, besides the little matter which I have just mentioned as indicating the family to which they belong, you have seen yourself that their plumage underneath is of a tawny-white colour, while above it is black streaked here and there with red. I noticed too that the one which flew off last had long, thin feathers growing out of his beak like a moustache, which is the characteristic sign of the male.'

"While chatting in this wise we entered the wood. The trees were filled with strange birds, who sang to us a concert of the most varied music.

"The youngsters, profiting by their last lesson, were preparing to fire; but I pointed out to them that the prodigious height of the trees upon which the gay singers were perched rendered any attempt at shooting useless.

"The form and the extraordinary girth of these gigantic trees struck us with astonishment. Their enormous trunks did not grow out of the ground like those of other trees, but were supported by powerful roots, which, lying exposed to the open air, rose into a kind of groined dome immediately under the tree, and thence ran out in all directions, dipping into the soil only here and there, and at a distance from the tree. Jack clambered up one of these roots, and measured the trunk with a piece of string. Ernest calculated that the girth of the tree could not be less than forty feet, while the height of the picturesque vault formed by some sixty of the roots, between the ground and the base of the trunk, was about eight feet.

"Nothing had ever struck me with greater admiration than the sight of this splendid vegetation. Ten or twelve trees alone formed that which we had hitherto supposed to be a wood. Their branches thrust themselves out to an incredible distance, and their foliage, which in shape reminded me of that of our own walnut-tree in Europe, threw a delicious shadow over a large extent of. Beneath, the earth was carpeted with a rich velvety greensward, which invited us to repose.

"We sat down. The provision-bags were opened. A stream which murmured along its pebbly course furnished us with clear spring-water, and the multitude of birds that sang over our heads gave to our repast the air of a festival. None of us lacked appetite.

"The place where we were seemed to me so excellently situated, that I did not think it worth while to seek further for a site for our future dwelling-place.

"I thereupon determined to return by the way we had come, and go down to the beach to try to collect whatever waifs from the wreck might have been cast up there by the wind and waves.

"Jack implored me, before setting out, to sew in the lining of his belt, which he had not ceased for an instant to carry in the sun as his brother had recommended, and which was now quite dry and fit for use.

"This done, he fastened the belt round his waist, stuck his pistols into it, and, looking as pleased as possible, strutted off to lead the way back and be the first to exhibit himself to you, in case you should have landed before our return. So anxious was he to get there, that we were obliged to hasten our steps in order that we might not lose sight of him.

"On the beach I found but few things to carry away, for most of the objects that we could reach were too heavy for our poor powers. While we were there, however, I noticed that the dogs were bounding along the edge of the water, and every now and then drawing out with their paws small crabs, which they devoured with relish.

"On quitting the beach we saw Fan scratch up the sand, and rake out a white-looking ball, which she swallowed greedily.

"'What if that were a turtle's egg?' cried Ernest.

"'Turtle's eggs!' said Francis. 'Are turtles fowls, then?'

"You may judge of the amusement which this question caused to Jack and Ernest.

"When the merriment had subsided, 'Let us profit by Fan's discovery,' said I; 'for I have heard say that these eggs are very nice to eat.'

"'They are indeed,' said Ernest, who was already rejoicing in thoughts that savoured of choice dishes.

"It was not without some difficulty that we drove Fan away from a repast which she found so much to her taste. Although she had already disposed of several eggs, there still remained about a score, which we carefully put away in our provision-bags.

"Then on looking out to sea, we caught sight of the sail of your boat. Francis feared that it might be a band of savages who were coming to kill us, but Ernest said he felt sure it was your vessel. And he was right; for a few minutes afterwards you came to land, and we were once more able to embrace each other.

"Such, my love, are our adventures. I sought a new dwelling-place—I have found one; and I am so delighted with it that, if you agree, we will set out tomorrow and establish our home beneath those magnificent trees. The view from it is superb, and the place itself is exquisite."

"What!" said I jestingly, "trees, good wife! Is that all that you have discovered towards a secure dwelling-place for us? I can quite understand, if they are as large as you say, that we could find a refuge in their branches in the night-time. But in order to get there we should require either wings or a balloon, which are not easy things to make or to manage."

"Ah!" said she, "you may laugh; but I am sure we could build an excellent cabin upon the branches of these trees, which could be reached easily enough by some wooden stairs. One often sees the same thing in Europe. Do you not remember, for instance, the linden in our own country, which has a cabin in its branches, and which for that reason is called 'Robinson's tree'?"

"All in good time," said I. "We can think over this difficult matter later on."

But night had already fallen: our conversation had caused us to forget the hour of repose. We offered up our nightly prayer, and at once retired to rest, in order that we might rise with the first beams of the morning sun.

CHAPTER 6

Removing—The Porcupine—The "Promised Land"

At the first dawning of day I woke up the children, to whom I
thought it right to give a few instructions concerning their duties
during our removal.

"We are going," I said, "to traverse a strange and, for aught I
know, dangerous tract of country. Let none of you venture alone.
The same risk menaces those who go too far ahead and those who
fall off in the rear. Let us all travel as closely together as we can, and
if an enemy presents itself, leave me to direct the attack or the
defence."

Morning prayer offered, and breakfast at an end, we prepared to
set out. The animals were driven in, and the ass and the cow were
loaded with the panniers which my wife had made on the previous
evening, and which we had filled with all such articles as were likely
to be of the greatest use to us. We took care, too, not to forget a little
of the captain's wine and some butter.

As I was about to complete the loading of the animals with our
bedclothes, our hammocks, and a quantity of cordage, my wife
interposed and claimed a seat for little Francis, as well as for the sack
which she called her enchanted bag. She also pointed out that it was
obviously necessary to take our fowls and pigeons with us, inasmuch
as they would most certainly disperse and be lost as soon as we ceased
to feed them. I gave way to her wishes. A comfortable place was
found for Francis on the back of the donkey, where he was safely
seated between the panniers, with the enchanted bag at his back to
lean against.

It now remained to catch the fowls and pigeons. The children ran
after them and did their best to capture them, but without taking a
single bird.

Wiser than they, my wife stood still, and told them that in that
position she would undertake to catch all the birds, scared as they
were, without any trouble whatever. "Ah, well!" said the youngsters,
"we shall see! we shall see!"

"I intend you to do so," replied their mother.

Upon that she scattered a few handfuls of grain around the entrance to the tent, and in a twinkling all our winged friends were around us. After they had eaten their first meal, she scattered a few more handfuls of grain, this time not outside, but inside the tent. Pigeons and fowls at once rushed in after it, and soon found themselves in a trap.

"More is to be done by address than by violence, you see, young gentlemen," said my wife, as she closed the entrance to the tent.

Jack was allowed to creep in to hold our feathered prisoners while we tied their legs together; and this done, we placed them on the back of the cow, shielding them from the sun with a cloth which we spread out upon a couple of sticks bent into the form of an arch. Thus hid away in the shade, they did not worry us with their cackling.

Everything we proposed to leave behind us that could be injured either by the rain or by the sun we shut up in the tent, the entrance to which we carefully closed up with stakes, and barricaded with casks and chests, some full and some empty.

Then I gave the signal to set out.

We were all well armed, and each of us carried a game-bag filled with provisions and ammunition. We were in the best of humours with ourselves and with each other.

Fritz, gun under arm, placed himself at the head of the procession. Behind him came my wife, leading in the cow and the ass, who walked side by side. On the latter was seated little Francis, who amused us greatly from time to time by his droll sayings. Behind the cow and the ass came Jack and the goat, and behind these Ernest and the sheep. I myself formed the rearguard. The dogs ran here, there, and everywhere, sniffing and barking, and constantly on the alert.

A few minutes later, the sow, which had at first appeared but little inclined to follow us, rejoined the party—not, however, without manifesting by her impatient gruntings the displeasure which so long a journey occasioned her. It may be as well to add that we did not trouble ourselves very seriously concerning her ill-humours.

We had not gone far when we saw our dogs bounding round a thicket, and barking excitedly, as if they were attacking some ferocious animal that had taken refuge there.

Fritz, with gun to shoulder and finger upon trigger, advanced resolutely to the charge.

Ernest uneasily took refuge nearer his mother; not, however, without making ready to fire should occasion require it.

Jack dashed intrepidly after his elder brother, with his gun slung carelessly over his shoulder.

I was hastening after to protect him if he should fall into danger when he cried out at the top of his voice, "Oh, papa! Come along! Make haste! A porcupine! an enormous porcupine!"

I hurried to the spot, and was not long in descrying what indeed was a porcupine, as Jack had said; but it was not nearly so large as he had given me to understand.

The dogs were still barking, and gnashing their teeth with rage to find themselves confronted by an animal which they could not attack without running the risk of paying dearly for their temerity.

The porcupine was carrying on the battle after the fashion of his tribe. He had turned tail upon his adversaries, and, with his head hidden between his paws, was thrusting himself backwards against them, with all his quills bristling and shaking in a manner which produced a strange rattling sound, that daunted the dogs as much as his odd method of fighting. Every time Turk or Fan pounced upon him they returned from the charge with a number of small but irritating wounds. At length their mouths and muzzles bled profusely.

Fritz and I stood watching for an opportunity to fire at the creature without danger of hurting the dogs.

Jack, however, more impatient, and not comprehending our hesitation, drew one of his pistols and, without more ado, shot the porcupine dead on the spot.

Jack, with his habitual lack of caution, had already laid hold upon the animal with his hands, and, in consequence, was bleeding from several wounds in them.

"Go and get a piece of string," said I; "you can then tie its feet together, and throw it over a stick, which you can carry between you, one holding each end."

But, impatient to show his game to his mother and younger brothers, Jack drew out his pocket-handkerchief, tied it round the neck of the porcupine, and dragged the animal along the ground to the place where the caravan awaited us.

Ernest, who now came up, examined the porcupine very attentively and with his usual deliberateness. He then remarked that it had in each jaw two long incisor teeth of the same kind as those of the hare and squirrel, while its ears were short and rounded, and had some distant resemblance to those of the human species.

My wife and I, meanwhile, had seated ourselves on the ground, and were engaged in drawing out the points of the creature's quills which still remained in the muzzles of our dogs.

Determined to carry the porcupine along with us, I placed round him a thick covering of herbs, and tied him up in some of our bed-clothes. I then fastened the bundle to the crupper of the donkey behind little Francis, and we proceeded upon our way.

At length, and without further adventure, we reached the "Promised Land".

"Magnificent!" cried Ernest, when he saw the huge trees which we were approaching; "what gigantic vegetation! The great spire of Strasburg is not nearly so high. How glorious are the works of nature, compared with those of man! What a delightful idea that was of mamma's, to quit the desolate place where we first put up our tent in order to live here!"

Then he asked me if I knew the names of these trees.

"So far as I am aware," I replied, "they are not described anywhere; and I have little doubt that we are the first Europeans who have been privileged to see them. I defy the most agile of bears to get at us when we have established our dwelling-place at the top of these huge bare trunks."

"So you like our trees now you come to see them for yourself?" said my wife.

"I can now understand why you admired them so," I replied. "I think your choice perfect."

"And yet you were so unhappy at the idea of leaving our old dwelling for this!" she said, pointing her finger at me playfully, and laughing. "Fie, incredulous man! You must see before you will condescend to believe, must you?"

I smilingly accepted the amicable reproach.

We halted. Our first care was to unload the beasts of burden, and turn them out to feed along with the sheep and the goat, first taking care to tie their fore-feet loosely together so that they might not stray away. The sow alone was left entirely mistress of her movements.

We then let out the fowls and pigeons. The fowls at once began picking insects out of the grass around us. The pigeons flew away into the branches of the trees, whence, however, they failed to descend at the first distribution of grain.

We then sat down upon the elastic greensward with which the whole soil thereabouts was carpeted, and took counsel together, concerning the construction of our house in one of the giant trees.

CHAPTER 7

The Tiger-Cat—The Wounded Flamingo

As it did not seem at all probable that we should be able to install ourselves in a new dwelling before the morrow, I became anxious concerning our means of passing the night in safety; for at present we were exposed to the weather, and had no defence against wild beasts.

I called Fritz, who I thought was among us, to tell him that I intended to attempt the ascent of one of the trees at once.

He made no reply; but two shots fired in succession, a short distance away, told us that he was not wasting his time. "Hit! hit! There he is!" we heard him crying excitedly.

In a few moments he made his appearance, carrying by the hindlegs a magnificent tiger-cat, which he proudly held up for us to look at.

"Bravo, my young hunter!" cried I; "you have rendered us a signal service in delivering our fowls and pigeons from this redoubtable neighbour; for they would not be safe from his clutches even if they were perched upon the topmost branches of these high trees."

"I found it close by," said Fritz. "I noticed something moving among the leaves of one of the trees, and going stealthily up to the foot of it, saw this creature among the branches. I fired at it, and it fell at my feet. As I was going to take it up, it got upon its feet, and was about to make off, when I brought it down dead with a pistol-shot."

"You may consider yourself fortunate," I replied, "that it did not, when you had only wounded it, fly at you instead of trying to run away. For these animals, although so small in build, are terrible when they are defending their lives. I can say this with the more certainty inasmuch as I think I now recognise in the animal which you have just killed, not the tiger-cat properly so-called, but the margay, or cayenne-cat, which is very common in South America, and is famous for its rapacity and audacity."

"However that may be," said Fritz, "look at its magnificent coat—at
47

those splendidly glossy black and brown spots upon the groundwork of gold! I trust Jack will be considerate enough to refrain from hacking the skin of my margay to pieces as he did that of my jackal."

"Never fear," said I. "If you only tell Jack that you want to keep a thing, he will not think of injuring it. But what do you propose to do with this skin?"

"I was just going to ask you what I should do with it," replied the young hunter. "I shall follow your advice in the matter. Let it be understood, also, that I have no wish to use it exclusively for my own benefit."

"Well said, my son," replied I. "In that case, as we have no need at present to draw upon furs for our clothing, I should advise that you turn the skin of the body and legs into cases for our silver dinner-sets which we found in the captain's cabin on the wreck, and that with the skin of the tail you make yourself a handsome hunting-belt to carry your knife and pistols in."

"And I, father?" asked Jack in his turn—"what shall I do with the skin of my porcupine?"

"Why, my boy," replied I, "after we have pulled out the quills to make needles or to tip arrows with, I fancy we shall be able to turn the skin into a kind of armour for the protection of our dogs in any future fights they may have with ferocious animals."

"Capital! capital!" cried Jack. "It will be great fun to see Turk and Fan dressed up in that fashion!"

And the impetuous fellow would give me no rest till I had shown him how to skin his porcupine.

To this end, I hung the animal up to a tree by the hind legs, and proceeded to flay him—an operation in which I succeeded to perfection.

Fritz, who watched me attentively, did the same by his margay.

We then nailed the two skins to the trunk of a tree to dry. A portion of the flesh of the porcupine was cut off for the repast which my wife was beginning to prepare; the rest was put by to be salted.

Ernest, meanwhile, had been collecting large stones, and building a fireplace, my wife was getting the dinner ready, and I was making needles out of the porcupine's quills. The point had been already made by nature; it only remained to pierce a hole through the other extremity, which I did with a long nail that I made red-hot in the fire. In a short time I turned out a large assortment of excellent needles, which my wife was very glad to accept.

The repast being at length ready, we seated ourselves around it on the grass, and fell-to. The flesh of the porcupine and the soup in which it had been boiled were found excellent, and we finished our meal with butter and Dutch cheese.

I told my wife to make us some straps as quickly as she could, in order that with these and a few lengths of rope we might go down to the beach and bring up what timber was necessary for our projected building operations. She set to work at once.

Meanwhile, I took the precaution to prepare our hammocks for the night, lest we should find ourselves without a bed to lie on. I hung them to the arched roots of one of the mangroves, and stretched a piece of sail-cloth over the top to preserve us both from the dew and the mosquitoes, of which latter there were swarms.

This done, I went down to the coast with Fritz and Ernest to see if we could find some pieces of wood that would serve for the steps of a ladder, which I intended to construct of stout cord.

Ernest discovered, at the edge of a morass, a quantity of bamboos which were half-buried in the ooze.

We pulled some of them up, and having cut them into lengths of three or four feet with our axes, made them up into three bundles—one for each of us.

At some distance from the place where we found the bamboos, and a little nearer the centre of the marsh I espied a thick bed of reeds, towards which I directed my steps in order to cut some for the purpose of making arrows of them. Fan, who was walking beside me, suddenly dashed forward, barking loudly; and immediately a flock of magnificent flamingoes flew off with extreme swiftness.

Fritz, who was never taken at unawares in emergencies of the kind, had just time to lift his gun to his shoulder and fire before the birds were out of range.

Two of the flamingoes fell—one of them stone dead, the other only wounded in the wing. This latter would in all probability have made good its escape, had not Fan at once bounded off in pursuit of it. She soon overtook it, and sagaciously held it by the wing until I came up and took it from her.

Desirous that the incident should not prevent me from taking possession of my coveted reeds, I set to work cutting a number of the longest of them, remarking to the boys that I intended to use them for measuring the height of the tree in which we proposed to build our habitation.

The two boys were silent.

Then, laden with our bamboos, our reeds, and the dead and the living flamingo—which latter I had tied by the legs—we returned to the family.

Jack and Francis welcomed the live flamingo with shouts of joy; but their mother looked troubled as she reflected that we were adding another useless mouth to the already large number of our domestic animals.

Less prone than she to be anxious on such a subject, I set myself to examine the creature's wounds. I saw that the ends of both its wings were fractured—in the one case by Fritz's gun-shot, in the other by the teeth of Fan. I dressed each of the wounds with a sort of ointment which I compounded of butter and salt and wine. This done, the flamingo was tied by a cord to a stake driven into the ground near the stream. Left to itself, it tucked its bill under its wing, supported itself upon one of its long legs, drawing the other close up to its body, and went off to sleep.

While I was engaged with my surgery, the youngsters had tied several reeds together, end to end, and were raising them against one of the mangroves to measure its height. Their measuring rod, however, scarcely reached to the place where the aerial roots sprang from the trunk; and I heard them expressing anew their doubts as to the success of the plan which I had hinted at, but had not yet explained to them.

Leaving them to their useless and incredulous gossip, and smiling at their perplexity, I took several of the reeds, which I pointed at one end, and garnished at the other with feathers plucked from the dead flamingo. I weighted the arrows thus formed by filling the hollow of the reed with sand. Then I constructed a bow by taking a bamboo-cane, shaving it off thin at each end, and drawing it into an arc with a piece of cord.

Jack and Fritz were not long in finding out what I was doing, then ran towards me, shouting, "Oh! a bow! a bow and arrows! Papa, let me shoot with it! Do let me try! You shall see that I know how to do it."

"One moment, children," I said. "Surely, if I have had the trouble of making the bow, I ought to have the honour of taking the first shot. Besides, do not suppose that I intend to use it merely as a toy. I have a useful end in view; and, if you will be patient an instant, I will show you what that end is."

I then asked my wife if she could find me a ball of coarse cotton.

"It is just possible that I may," she replied with a smile. "I will consult my enchanted bag."

She put her hand into the bag and drew it out again, saying, "There, that is the article I think you require."

Having unwound the greater part of the ball of cotton, I fastened the end of it to one of the arrows. Then, adjusting the arrow upon the bow, I drew in the direction of that part of the highest mangrove where we proposed to build our new dwelling. The shaft fell on the other side of one of the branches, upon which, therefore, the cotton hung suspended.

It was easy enough now, by drawing the arrow back to the branch, to get a length of cotton equal to the height of our intended domicile, and thus to judge of the length of ladder it would be necessary to construct.

We found that we should want one about fifty feet long. I measured off something like a hundred feet of strong cord, which I divided into two parts, and laid out in parallel lines upon the ground. I then told Fritz to saw the bamboos into lengths of two feet each, and, assisted by Jack and Ernest, I placed these ladder-wise between the ropes, and fastened them at each end—first with a knot to fix their position, and then with a nail to prevent them from slipping.

In less than an hour and a half the ladder was finished. In order to hoist it into its place, I employed the same means which had served me so well in measuring the height. Another arrow was shot off. The cotton lodged as before. But to the first thread I had attached a triple one, to that a piece of twine, to that a strong cord, and to that the ladder. All I had to do, therefore, was to pull the arrow-end of the cotton until I had drawn the ladder into its place. I then had the strong cord to fasten it by to one of the arched roots of the mangroves, and our stairs were complete.

Jack and Fritz fell into a dispute as to who should first ascend. I gave the preference to Jack, who was lighter than his brother, and as agile as a mouse. Before allowing him to start, however, I advised him not to venture a single step until he had ascertained that the rung of the ladder upon which he was next to tread was solidly fixed and strong enough to bear his weight. I also counselled him to come down as swiftly as he could on perceiving the least danger.

He instantly commenced the ascent, paying very little attention to my recommendations, and in a few moments reached—Heaven be thanked, without accident!—the first branch, across which he seated himself astride as upon a horse, shouting:

"Victory! victory!"

Fritz was the next to mount. With a few pieces of rope he made the ladder still more secure, and I then hazarded the ascent myself.

Landed safely among the branches, I took a careful survey of the whole trunk at that part, with a view of fixing upon the best spot for our future habitation.

Night fell suddenly while I was thus employed, but by the light of the moon I managed to fix to one of the branches a large pulley which I had brought with me; and this served in the morning to enable us to draw up our building materials.

Our careful housewife, who had milked the cow and the goats, gave us some excellent porridge, and afterwards brought out the remainder of the porcupine left from dinner. We made a hearty meal.

We tied up the beasts near our hammocks beneath the arched roots of the great tree.

Ernest and Francis had employed the time we had spent aloft by gathering together, in accordance with my instructions, a great quantity of dead wood, which enabled me to keep in a large bonfire all night for the purpose of frightening away the wild beasts.

Our evening prayer being offered, my wife and the children were not long in getting to rest in the hammocks which swung from the over-hanging roots.

For myself, I rested not. I had resolved to keep watch, so that our fire might not go out while we slept.

CHAPTER 8

The Building in the Tree

Immediately after breakfast my wife ordered Jack and Ernest to
harness the ass and the cow with the straps which, under my
instructions, she had made on the previous evening. Then, with the
three younger boys, she made preparations for a journey to the
beach to bring up what timber might be necessary for the construction of our aerial habitation. When she had set out I ascended the
tree with Fritz, and chose a spot in the centre of the lower branches,
where, aided by saw and axe, we prepared a place for the erection of
our hut. The branches themselves, spreading out horizontally,
served us to a thought as joists for our flooring. We left a few some
six or eight feet above these on which to hang our hammocks. A few
others a little higher were so trimmed as to form rafters for the
support of our sail-cloth, which was to be used for roofing.

These preliminary preparations were not achieved without difficulty; but in the end we had the happiness of finding that we had
cleared a large open space in the thick branches of the mangrove,
which would serve us admirably as a site for a dwelling-house.

The beams and planks, which had in the meantime been brought
in large quantities from the beach, were now drawn up into the tree
by the pulley—a contrivance which multiplied our strength even
more than we had anticipated.

The floor was laid, and a hand-rail placed all round it.

We worked with so much ardour, that the middle of the day
overtook us before we had one thought of eating.

We contented ourselves with a light lunch, and after the repast
returned with renewed vigour to our task.

Our first business was to stretch our sail-cloth across the higher
branches—a labour requiring not a little address and exertion. We
finally decided to draw it over one branch and fasten it to the
handrail on either side, thus forming a kind of gable. This done, our
hut, of which the huge trunk of the tree formed one of the walls, was
hermetically closed on three of its sides. The fourth, which faced the
sea, was left open for the present, but I had hit upon a plan of

53

closing it in case of need. I determined to cover it with another sail-cloth fixed upon a roller like a blind, so that we could draw it up or pull it down at will.

When we had slung our hammocks to the branches which we had left for that purpose our habitation was ready for occupation at night.

The sun was already sinking to rest.

Fritz and I descended from the tree; and, although I was very tired, I at once set to work upon the remaining planks and posts, and constructed a table and some seats upon the site of our late dwelling-place. It seemed to me a fitting spot for our future diningroom.

The last labour accomplished to the intense satisfaction of the whole family, I threw myself, worn out with fatigue, upon one of the benches I had just constructed. Wiping my forehead, which was bathed in perspiration, I said to my wife, "I have worked today like a negro, and I will rest the whole of tomorrow."

"I agree," said my wife. She then called the boys, who, though scattered in all directions, were not long in hastening in and seating themselves around the table upon which dinner was already laid.

After dinner we ascended the tree. Fritz, Jack, and Ernest went first, and accomplished the ascent with the agility of cats. Their mother followed, slowly and with the utmost precaution.

Left to the last, I had a little more difficulty than the others, for I had thought it wise to unfasten the ladder from its stake at the lower end, in order that I might draw it up after me; moreover, I carried tied to my back our little Francis, whom I did not like to trust alone.

I reach my destination without mishap, and when I had drawn up the ladder, the boys compared our new dwelling-place to one of those enchanted castles of ancient chivalry which were impregnable to all assaults.

However that might be, I did not neglect to load the arms in readiness to fire upon any ill-intentioned visitor. Our dogs keeping guard at the foot of the tree would signal the enemy's approach: we could do the rest ourselves.

Our precautions thus taken, each retired to his hammock. Sleep fell upon all of us, and the night flowed by in sweet tranquillity.

CHAPTER 9

Sunday

Morning.

Jack begged me to lend him my bow, which I did. Shortly afterwards I found him endeavouring to tip his arrows with porcupine quills.

I advised him to melt one of the soup-cakes in a small quantity of water, and see if that would serve the purpose.

He adopted my suggestion, and soon had the satisfaction of finding himself armed with a number of arrows which would be deadly in the hands of a skilful archer.

Fritz, who had decided to use up the skin of his margay in the manufacture of cases for our dinner sets, as I had recommended, came to consult me upon the best means of currying his leather.

I advised him to rub it with ashes and sand, and to soften it afterwards with butter and the yolks of eggs.

While Fritz was engaged in his amateur currying operations, Francis, already the possessor of a small bow and arrows, which he was learning to shoot with skill, came to me to beg that I would make him a quiver, which he could sling over his shoulder and use for carrying the arrows I had made for him from the reeds. I made him one with four pieces of bark cut off to a point and nailed neatly together. Thus equipped, the infant Nimrod set out joyously in search of adventure.

It was not long before my wife called us to our dinner.

While we were dining I told my boys that I desired to lay before them a very important proposition.

Their eyes were all fixed upon me at once with the utmost curiosity.

"It is," I said, "to give names to the various points of the island which we have visited and become acquainted with. By the aid of these names we shall be the better able to understand each other in conversation, and shall not have to use so many words to describe where we have been or intend to go. We will abstain, however," I added, "from giving names to places on the coast, for it is not unlikely that European navigators have already discovered and christened them, and in that case we must be careful to respect the work of our predecessors."

"A capital idea! an excellent thought!" cried all the children at once. "Let us invent some names on the spot."

"To commence with the bay where we debarked from the wrecked vessel, I propose that we call it Deliverance Bay," said Ernest.

"Agreed! agreed! Deliverance Bay!" they all cried in unison.

All the points in our domain received names in succession. The place of our first habitation was called Undertent; the small island in the bay Shark Island, in memory of the courage and address of Fritz. Then came Flamingo Marsh and Jackal River. Our new dwelling-place received the name of Falcon-nest; "for," said I to my boys, "you are as hardy and adventurous as young falcons, and as much disposed to deeds of pillage in the immediate neighbourhood of your home." The promontory from the top of which Fritz and I had vainly sought far and wide for traces of our unfortunate fellow-voyagers was named Cape Disappointment.

These useful designations fixed upon, we rose from table and each of the boys was again set free to amuse himself as he listed.

Fritz still busied himself in the manufacture of cases for the dinner sets. He fashioned four out of the feet of the skin, thrusting in a wooden mould which he had made to give them the proper form.

Jack begged me to assist him in getting ready for Turk the coat of mail which I had previously suggested should be made out of the thorny skin of the porcupine.

After having cleaned the skin in the same manner as I had recommended to Fritz for his margay, we fastened it with straps to the back and breast and shoulders of the dog, who, thus decked out, wore an aspect altogether warlike. He was very docile while we harnessed him, and appeared to have no thought of disembarrassing himself of his strange armour.

Fan, however, was far from finding her companion's costume to her taste. Every time she approached him, as her habit was, to caress and sport with him, she returned from the charge with a cruelly-punctured hide. She was puzzled. Thereupon it was sagely decided that war trappings were not a thing to be abused, and that Master Turk should only be fitted out with his coat of mail when we were about to engage in expeditions of the first importance.

The sun was now past the meridian: the heat had decreased. I proposed to walk. We deliberated upon the direction we should take, and for several reasons fixed upon Undertent. Certain of our

THE SWISS FAMILY ROBINSON

provisions were running short, and it was thought well to look to our magazines. Fritz and Jack wanted powder and shot. My wife wanted butter. Ernest hit upon the idea of bringing home a couple of the ducks, which he explained would find good water in the stream that ran beneath Falcon-nest.

"Let us set out at once, then," said I, "and prepare yourselves for a little fatigue. We are going to take a longer route than that by which we came."

We were soon on our way. Fritz and Jack, armed, as I and Ernest were, with their guns, took the lead—the one decorated with his jackal-skin-belt, the other in a newly-made porcupine helmet. Even little Francis carried his bow and quiver. My wife alone was unarmed.

The monkey, who insisted on being of the party, leapt precipitately to his accustomed seat upon the back of Turk; but finding himself sorely pinched by the spikes of the dog's new coat of mail, put on for the occasion, took refuge upon the crupper of Fan, who benevolently consented to give the impudent little cavalier a mount.

Our flamingo, who also desired to be of the party, put himself gravely at the tail of the caravan. He was a droll addition to our company, marching wide upon his stilts, and curving his long neck as he went. I think it right to say that he looked incontestably the most reflective and self-satisfied of the whole troupe.

Coasting the stream—Falcon-nest Stream—we fell into a most agreeable route. My wife and I walked slowly side by side. The boys ran on before, wandering now to the right and now to the left.

Before long Ernest came running towards us, holding in his hand a stalk, from which depended three or four small balls of a light green colour, and crying out, "Potatoes, papa! I have found some potatoes!"

I had no difficulty in pronouncing his judgment to be accurate, and I could not refrain from commending his spirit of inquiry and observation, which in this instance had resulted in the most important discovery we had made since our sojourn on the island.

Ernest, in a glow of gratified excitement, pressed us to make all haste to a spot whence he would show us a larger potato-field than we had ever yet seen; "for," said he, "at the place where I gathered this stalk the whole plain is covered with potatoes."

We were not slow in making our way to this precious natural plantation. Jack at once threw himself upon his knees, and commenced grubbing up the earth to get at the potatoes. The monkey, leaping off Fan's back, failed not to imitate its young master. In less than five minutes they brought to light between them a large quantity of excellent fruit, which Francis piled in heaps as fast as Nip and Jack threw them upon the ground.

The whole of the potatoes thus obtained were stowed away in our bag, and we resumed our journey, after carefully observing the situation of the field; for we had resolved to return next day and complete the harvest.

We crossed the stream at the foot of a little chain of boulders, over which the water poured in the form of a cascade. Not only was the fall itself charming, but the view all round was as varied and beautiful as it was extensive. We might have fancied ourselves in a European hot-house, except that the flower-pots and the stages on which they stand were replaced by pile on pile of broken rocks, from whose fissures sprang plants of the most magnificent descriptions, both in beauty and dimensions. There were also the Indian fig-tree, the aloe, the cactus, with its prickly stalk and flame-red bloom; the plantain, with its long, sinuous arms endlessly interlaced; and, though last not least, the anana, bearer of the most delicious of fruits. The boys, assisted by Ernest, quickly recognised the latter, and applied themselves to its appetising treasures with an avidity which I was obliged to repress. I feared they might make themselves ill.

Among other plants, I lighted upon the karata, a kind of aloe, of which I gathered several sprigs. Showing them to the children, I said, "See here! I have found a treasure far superior to the anana, which you have been devouring so greedily."

"What!" cried Jack, with his mouth full, "those scrubby-looking bunches of leaves? Impossible! There can be nothing there like the anana. The anana is the fruit for me."

"Gluttonous boy!" I said, interrupting his panegyric, of which I saw by their looks the other boys highly approved; "it is necessary that you should learn not to judge by appearances. See here, Ernest—you are the most sensible of the four—take this steel and the flint of my gun, and give me a light: I want one particularly."

"But, father," replied the young savant, looking perplexed. "I have neither a sulphur match nor touchwood; how am I to get a light?"

"How should we proceed," exclaimed I, "if it was necessary to get a light at all hazards?"

"Well," replied Jack, "I have heard that when savages are in a similar difficulty they procure a light by rubbing two pieces of wood together till they burn. I suppose we should have to do the same."

"A tiresome and barren method for people not accustomed to so painful an exercise!" I exclaimed. "I think I may safely venture to tell you that you would have to rub for days without getting a single spark."

"In that case," said Ernest, "I suppose we shall be compelled to search for touchwood."

"Such a search," said I, "is superfluous." And I took a dry twig of the karata, from which I peeled off the bark and extracted the pith. Then I laid the pith upon the gun-flint, and struck it a smart blow with the steel. The first stroke set the substance on fire.

"Hurrah! hurrah!" cried the children in astonishment, "a touch-wood tree! a touchwood tree!"

"You are surprised thus far," I said, "but you have not yet seen half the usefulness that lies concealed beneath the bark of this wonderful plant."

As I spoke I stripped off one of the leaves, from which I drew out several lengths of a very strong though very fine thread.

"Really," said Jack, "the karata is a far more valuable plant than I had supposed. But these thorny things that lie scattered all around us can be of no possible use."

"You are altogether in the wrong," I replied, "in concluding so hastily that these are useless. The aloe, for instance, produces a juice which is very much used in medicine. Then there is the Indian fig, with its battledore-shaped leaves. This plant grows in the most arid soils, where, but for the timely succour of its fruit, many a weary traveller would be in danger of perishing by hunger."

At these words Jack dashed among the foliage to gather some of the fruit, which he was impatient to taste; but the long prickles with which they were covered pierced his hands in all directions, and he returned crestfallen and crying, regarding the fig-tree with a look of unmitigated disgust.

His mother hastened to remove the thorns from his fingers, and while she was thus employed I showed the other children how to pluck and eat the fruit without running so much risk.

Having taken a short stick and pointed it, I stuck the sharp end in-to one of the figs, which I could then harmlessly skin with my knife.

Ernest, who, so soon as this was done, examined the fruit attentively, ascertained that it was covered with myriads of small insects, which appeared to be spending their time in sucking its juice.

"Do look here, papa," he said, "and tell me what these little creatures are. I think I know something about them, but I may be in error."

I at once recognised the cochineal, and exclaimed, "Fortunate in the extreme! We have certainly lighted upon a day of discoveries. I am not sure, indeed, that this last is not the most precious that we have yet made, though to make proof of that we ought to be able to traffic with the people of Europe, who buy cochineal at a very costly rate, to make a scarlet dye."

"However that may be," said Ernest, "we have at least found a second plant which is superior to the anana, of which we at first boasted so much."

"You are right," I replied, "and to prove it I will tell you of yet another use to which the Indian fig may be put. Its dense prickly leaves make excellent hedges to protect dwellings against the attacks of savages, and plantations against those of beasts of prey."

"What!" cried Jack, "these tender leaves serve the purpose of a barrier against animals! Why, with the cut of a knife, or the stroke of a stick, I could demolish them at once."

With that he began to slash away vigorously at a large fig-tree.

But one of its battledore-leaves struck his leg, and pierced him with its spikes till he roared again.

"Ah! ah!" laughed I. "Do you understand now how it is that an enclosure of these trees may prove impregnable to half-clad savages, and to animals that try to break through them with no other weapons but those furnished them by Nature?"

"We must plant a hedge of them round Falcon-nest," said Ernest.

"And I think," added Fritz, "that we should collect as many cochineal insects as possible. Their red dye may be of use to us some day."

"So far as I am concerned," I said, "I think it would be far wiser to confine ourselves to works of utility. The agreeable must be reserved for a future occasion, Master Fritz."

Arrived at Jackal River, we crossed it without difficulty, and after a few minutes' walk found ourselves at Undertent, where all remained in the order in which we had left it.

Fritz furnished himself abundantly with powder and lead. I helped my wife to fill her tin flask with butter. The younger children endeavoured to catch the ducks, which had become wilder than heretofore, and would not allow themselves to be approached.

Ernest, determined to capture them, adopted a stratagem which succeeded to perfection. To the end of a piece of string, he attached a morsel of cheese, and let it float upon the water. The greedy birds soon darted after the bait and swallowed it and then Ernest had no difficulty in drawing them gently to the edge of the river. By dint of repeating this manoeuvre several times he made himself master of the rebels. Once taken, they were each tied up securely in a handkerchief, and thus enveloped were placed in our gamebags.

We next took in a supply of salt from the cave, though we did not get so much as we wanted, for we were too heavily loaded already.

We were even obliged to relieve Turk of his coat of mail, and make him for the time being a beast of burden.

The redoubtable but scarcely useful cuirass was left in the tent.

"It is the same with armour as with soldiers," said Ernest; "when there is no fighting to be done it is good for nothing."

We set out for Falcon-nest again. The laughter and fun provoked by the contortions of our feathery prisoners, and the comic aspect of our caravan, helped us to forgetfulness of the weight of our burdens. It was not until the journey was ended that we felt fatigued.

Our good housewife at once filled our pot with potatoes, and while we made up the fire, she milked the cow and the goat, in order to prepare for us our evening repast.

Our table was soon spread.

The expectation of a good supper, and of partaking of the potatoes, which formed the dish of honour, kept us awake; but as soon as the meal was finished, the children were glad to retire to their hammocks.

In a few minutes profound slumber fell upon our household.

CHAPTER 10

The Sledge—The Salmon—The Kangaroo

I had remarked during our journey to Undertent that the beach was covered with a quantity of pieces of wood, which I thought were suitable for the construction of a kind of sledge, with the assistance of which we might be able to transport such articles as were too heavy for the backs of our beasts.

So I set out at daybreak to bring some of them home, accompanied by Ernest and by the donkey, both of whom I was obliged to awaken, so soundly did they sleep.

The sledge took less than an hour to construct.

At the point of starting, Fritz presented us with a margay-skin sheath, which would either hold a knife and fork or a small axe. I praised his ingenuity and industry; and having embraced the rest of the family, Ernest and I set out.

The ass and the cow were harnessed to the sledge. Ernest and I, armed with a bamboo cane each to supply the place of whips, and carrying our guns slung to our backs, walked one on each side of our new conveyance. Fan followed us.

We took the road leading by the stream, and after a journey entirely unmarked by adventure, we came to Undertent.

The beasts were detached and set free, while we loaded our sledge with the firkin of butter, a barrel of powder, bullets, cheese, and other provisions.

I felt that a bath would refresh us both after the fatigue of the day. Thereupon, I went down to Deliverance Bay and soon succeeded in finding a place where the rocks rose in clusters from a bottom of fine sand, forming, so far as privacy was concerned, a long row of natural bathing-rooms.

I swam in the water something like half an hour, and then, as Ernest did not put in an appearance, I dressed myself and went to seek him. I had scarcely gone a hundred steps when I heard him crying out—

"Father! father! Pray come and help me! Make haste, or he will drag me in!"

I ran, and soon came in sight of our young philosopher lying prone on the sand, not far from the mouth of the river, and holding with both hands a line, at the end of which an enormous fish was struggling with all its might.

I came up just in time to spare the ambitious fisherman the anguish of seeing his magnificent capture escape him; for he was breathless, and his strength was well-nigh exhausted.

I took the string and drew the fish into a shallow, where it was easy enough to take him—especially after Ernest had waded into the water and stunned him with a blow of his axe.

It was a salmon, weighing at least fifteen pounds.

I opened the fish, and sprinkled it with salt, to keep it fresh. I then packed it in the sledge with some other fish of various sizes which Ernest had also caught and had tied up in his handkerchief.

This done, I replaced the planks in the bridge; and when my son returned, we harnessed the beasts and retraced our steps to Falcon-nest.

We had been walking about a quarter of an hour, and were making our way along the prairie, when all at once Fan dashed barking towards a clump of tall grasses. Immediately there rushed out of the clump an animal nearly as large as a sheep, which made its way off, not by running, but by a series of extraordinary bounds. I fired—too hastily, however—and I missed.

Ernest, warned by my shot, and being at the time nearer the fugitive than I was, fired also, and killed it on the spot.

We hastened to examine the strange game which we had thus bagged.

The creature's coat and muzzle were like those of the mouse, its ears like a rabbit's, its tail like a tiger's, its forelegs very short, and its hind-legs excessively long. I examined it for a long time and could not tell what it was.

As to Ernest, the pleasures of victory left him no time to make his accustomed investigations. He was wholly occupied with the important achievement of having killed the creature.

"Oh!" he cried, in an ecstasy, "what will my mother and my brothers say when they see game of this size, and learn that it was I alone who killed it?"

"Truly," I said, "you have a good eye and a sure hand; but I should very much like to know the name of the animal. Let us make a minute examination of it, and perhaps we shall arrive at some——"

Ernest interrupted me.

"It has," he said, "four incisor teeth, and therefore it must belong to the rodent order of animals."

"Well reasoned," replied I; "but it also has a pouch below the breast, and that is a distinctive sign of the Marsupialia. And if I am not very much deceived, I think we shall find ourselves the possessors of a female kangaroo, an animal unknown to naturalists until the discovery of New Holland by the celebrated Captain Cook, who was the first to examine and describe it. You may, therefore, flatter yourself that you have brought down an extraordinary head of game."

The kangaroo was placed upon the sledge, and as we proceeded on our way I told Ernest all I knew about the animal, of its forelegs which were too short, of its hind-legs which were too long, and of its tail which, as a kind of compensation for its inequalities of limb, served its purpose almost as well as a fifth leg.

As soon as the children left at Falcon-nest saw us coming they shouted for joy, and ran to meet us. As they came in sight we could not help laughing heartily: they were so comically attired. One was enveloped in a long white shirt; the body of another was concealed up to the armpits in a pair of huge blue trousers; the third was habited in a waistcoat which came down to his knees, and gave him the appearance of a walking portmanteau.

Seeing them thus attired, walking towards us with the gravity and solemnity of theatrical heroes, I desired them to tell me the cause of this masquerade.

They replied that during our absence their mother had thought it proper to wash their clothes, and that until these were dry they had been obliged to dress themselves in what they could find among the contents of the chest, which I had turned into a sledge.

After we had minutely inspected and laughed long and loudly at their strange accoutrements, they passed round the sledge to examine its contents.

Our housewife failed not to thank us warmly for the butter, the salt, and the fish we had brought; but the attention of the children was concentrated wholly upon the salmon and the kangaroo, which Ernest exhibited with no little pride.

The sledge being unloaded, I made a distribution of salt among the animals, who had gone without for some time, and enjoyed their feast immensely.

The kangaroo was hung up to a neighbouring branch, and we sat down to a supper consisting of the small fish caught by Ernest and a dish of potatoes.

Night fell, and we retired to our aerial dwelling-place.

CHAPTER 11

A Second Voyage to the Vessel—The Turtle—Tapioca

The next morning, very early, I called Fritz, and told him that I desired him to accompany me again on a voyage to the wrecked vessel.

I then descended from the tree and employed myself in denuding the kangaroo of his beautiful grey skin. The flesh I divided into two portions—the one to be eaten fresh, the other to be salted for future use.

We breakfasted, and after the repast I told Fritz to furnish our gamebags with food and our gourd-bottles with drink, and to make ready such arms as we should require to take with us.

Soon afterwards our tub-boat was drifting swiftly with the current towards the vessel, which we reached without accident.

My first care was to seek for materials with which to construct a raft, upon which, in accordance with a plan laid down by Ernest on the preceding evening, we could bear to land a much heavier load than our boat was capable of carrying.

I had the good fortune to find between decks a large quantity of empty water-casks. We picked out a dozen of them which we fastened together with pieces of wood strongly nailed to the tubstaves. I then made a flooring of planks, and surrounded the whole with a handrail about two feet high.

This work occupied us during the greater part of the day. At all events, when we had finished it, it was too late to hope to return to land with our new construction properly loaded.

This being so, we determined to make a tour of inspection all over the vessel, and take an inventory of what we judged it best to carry ashore. We then retired to the captain's cabin, and after a frugal repast, the sweet restorer—sleep—overtook us as we lay at full length upon a couple of excellent mattresses.

The next morning at daybreak we were afoot refreshed by our night's rest and in good health and spirits.

We at once set about building our boats. The apartment in which we had slept was the first to be stripped. Our second visit was made to the cabin we had ourselves occupied during our unfortunate voyage. I brought from thence everything that was useful or had an interest for us as a souvenir of bygone days. The other cabins we took in turn.

Locks, bolts, window-fastenings, the windows themselves, even the doors were taken off and made ready for transport. Two trunks abundantly furnished with necessaries were among the booty; but what gave me the greatest pleasure of all was to find two larger chests, one filled with carpenter's tools and the other with those of a gunsmith. A casket containing gold and silver watches, snuffboxes, rings, and other valuables dazzled us for an instant; but our attention was soon drawn more seriously towards a large store of oats, peas, and maize, and a number of European fruit-trees, which were carefully preserved for planting on the distant continent to which the doomed vessel was directing her course when she was wrecked.

But what was our joy to find, besides these, a stock of iron bars, wheels, pickaxes, and spades, and above all a hand-mill! Nothing which could be of use in a young colony had been forgotten in fitting out this vessel which was to have borne us to the New World. We could not bear everything away. A coffer full of coin scarcely attracted our attention. Of what value was money to us when compared with the rude implements which would supply our first necessities? From the jewellery casket we took the two watches which we had promised to the younger children, and from the coinchest a handful of coins; it was all we removed of that which is conventionally called valuable.

Fritz begged me to let him take a fishing-net, a pair of harpoons, and a reel of line which he found by chance.

I gave him permission.

Our loading occupied us half the day. At length the time for setting out for the shore arrived. It was not without considerable difficulty that we got our over-charged boats in motion. Happily a favourable wind came to our aid, filling the sail that I had spread.

I was at the helm. The sail, bellied well to the breeze, prevented me from seeing what Fritz was doing in the fore part of the vessel. All at once I heard the whistling of the reel of line as it ran swiftly out of the boat.

"Great heaven, Fritz!" I cried; "what are you doing?"

"Struck! struck!" cried he, in a transport of joy. "She can never escape that!"

His exclamations referred to an enormous turtle which he had perceived sleeping upon the surface of the water and had bravely and adroitly harpooned.

The animal, pierced in the neck, darted off, drawing our boat after it at a terrific speed.

I struck sail hastily, and rushed to the prow of the vessel to cut the line of the harpoon; but Fritz entreated me not to permit so splendid a prey to escape, assuring me that he would cut the line himself if he found ourselves in the least danger.

Thus conducted by the animal, we cut through the water with incredible swiftness, and I had the greatest difficulty in handling the rudder in such a manner as to neutralise the effects of the strange motion which our singular tug gave to the vessel. Perceiving at length that the turtle was directing his course towards the open sea, I hoisted sail again. The wind was blowing inshore, and the animal, finding the resistance too great, changed his course and swam landwards.

We touched the bottom within gunshot of the shore opposite Falcon-nest. I leapt into the sea with the intention of finishing the turtle with my axe, but the creature had run head first into the sand, and was stranded. At the first stroke of the axe I severed its head from its body.

Fritz, delighted beyond measure at his achievement, fired a gun to advise the family of our return, and in a few moments they were all running down to the beach to meet us.

Then Fritz told the story of the turtle.

His mother trembled as she heard the record of the danger to which we had been exposed; and all expressed their admiration at the skill Fritz had displayed in taking such excellent aim at the precise part of the animal which, as Ernest explained, was always protected by the carapace, or vaulted back-shell of the animal except when its wearer was asleep.

The two younger children were sent up to Falcon-nest to fetch the beasts of burden, with which they soon returned, having in the meantime harnessed them to the sledge. Upon this primitive means of transport we placed our mattresses and the turtle, which together weighed somewhere about three quintals: it required our united strength to lift them. The remainder of the cargo was carried up the beach beyond the reach of the tide, and our tub-boat and raft were anchored by means of large lumps of lead buried in the sand.

Arrived at Falcon-nest, I at once set to work to remove the turtle from its shell. Then I cut off some steaks from its flesh, which I desired my wife to broil for supper.

"Well, my dear Fritz," said I, "how do you propose to make use of your carapace?"

"I think," he said, "that I should make a tank of it, so that my mother could always have a supply of fresh water without going down to the stream for it."

"An excellent idea," I cried, "and one which must be put into execution as soon as we can find some clay to set our tank in."

"When the tank is put in its place," said Ernest, assuming his scholarly air, "I shall take leave to set some roots in it which I have found today. They appear to me to be a species either of the common radish or of horseradish."

After examining them carefully: "If I am not mistaken," I said, "you have made a most valuable discovery, which, added to the potato field, will always preserve us from famine. I believe I recognise in these roots those of the tapioca plant, with which the Indians of the West make a species of bread called cassava. But in order to be put to this use, it is necessary that the root should undergo a process which shall remove from it a certain poisonous substance that it contains."

This conversation did not prevent us from setting vigorously to work to unload the sledge.

As soon as this was done, I made another journey to the beach to bring up a second load before nightfall. My wife remained behind, in company with little Francis, who never disdained to play the part of scullion, being well assured by previous experience that he would become the possessor of some choice tit-bit during the preparation of the meal. I told his mother and him in setting out that we expected to reap the reward of our labours in a right royal feast.

Arrived at the raft, the sledge was loaded with a mass of articles, of which the hand-mill, by reason of the discovery of the tapioca-root, appeared to me to be by far the most useful.

This labour achieved, my wife called us to supper.

Fritz's turtle, excellently cooked, was enjoyed by all of us.

"It's an ugly brute, is that turtle," said little Francis as he went to his new bed, "but it was very nice to eat—eh, Jack?"

Jack was fast asleep.

Our mattresses had done their work.

CHAPTER 12

The Onager—Flax—The Rainy Season

One morning as we were about beginning work, we were startled by a series of the most extraordinary noises, which seemed to be borne upon the wind from a distance. They consisted mainly of a sort of howling, which was mingled with hissing and whistling, and ended in a succession of lamentable wails.

Fearing a hostile attack, we hastened to drive our animals beneath the arched roots of our tree, and then took to our castle among the branches. Our dogs, pricking up their ears, put themselves on the alert.

Perfect silence lasted for some minutes, and then the strange noises were heard again—this time much nearer and louder.

We were all looking anxiously in the direction whence the unknown sounds proceeded, when all at once Fritz, who had sharper eyes than the rest of us, threw aside his gun and, bursting into a loud laugh, cried, "It is our donkey, and he is giving a flourish of trumpets to signalise his return! What delightful music, to be sure! Liberty seems to have improved his voice!"

The other boys looked piqued at being alarmed by so trivial a cause.

I felt less assurance than any of them.

"It is not at all unlikely," I said, "that our ass may have something to do with this extraordinary music; but he could hardly make so much noise alone."

"You are right, father," said Fritz, who was still looking out among the trees, "for I see now that he is bringing company with him."

I looked in the direction indicated by Fritz, and saw a magnificent onager, or wild ass, trotting along by our own Longears and braying hideously.

Without delay I cast about for some means of capturing the beast. I descended softly from the tree, followed by Fritz, cautioning the boys meanwhile to remain where they were, and make as little noise as possible.

I then took a long rope, one end of which I tied to one of the roots of the tree, while in the other I tied a slip-knot, inserting a small stick to keep it open.

With a piece of bamboo I made a sort of cleft-stick, of which Fritz, who was very curious on the subject, tried in vain to guess the use. In his impatience to catch the onager he wanted to use the lasso; but I stopped him, observing that my plan, which was the Patagonian one, would prove the better on this occasion.

Fritz fell in with my views, and I instructed him how to proceed.

As the two animals approached the tree the onager caught sight of us, and as ours were probably the first human faces he had ever seen, he started back affrighted.

Fritz held out to our donkey a handful of oats. Master Longears was not too well fed to resist temptation. He ran up so fast that the onager, judging there was something worth having in the wind, followed him without mistrust.

I profited by the opportunity to slip my noose over his neck, by means of a pole at the end of which I held it.

Immediately the onager made a sharp bound backwards, and was turning to fly, when the knot closed round his neck, and the rope brought him up so suddenly that he fell to the ground as if suffocated.

I hastened to loosen the cord, lest it should kill him, and replaced it by the halter of our own donkey. Then, before he could recover himself, I closed his nostrils with my bamboo cleft-stick, the open ends of which I tied tightly together with a piece of string, thus employing to tame the animal the method adopted by farriers when they have to shoe a vicious horse.

This done, I fastened the halter with two long ropes to the roots of our tree, and waited for the captive to come to his senses again, in order to see what more was necessary to be done to bring him into complete subjection.

At the end of a few minutes the animal leapt up and made a brave struggle to regain his liberty. The bamboo cleft-stick, however, troubled him exceedingly, and considerably damped his ardour, so that before long he became quiet enough to be led to the place that served us for a stable.

This accomplished, it became necessary to take measures to prevent another desertion on the part of our own donkey, our confidence in whose fidelity was very naturally shaken. Having fettered his fore-legs, I tied him up beside the onager, thinking that his enforced society might be a means of teaching the new animal the kind of life he would be expected to lead in future.

We found it no easy task to train our onager. We condemned him to privations and even to blows, but we could do nothing with him until we adopted the American plan of clipping his ears. This finished his education.

At the end of a few weeks, Lightfoot—this was the name we gave him—was so well broken in that we were able to mount him without fear. In order to manoeuvre him, I attached to his halter a sort of cavesson, or noseband, into which I fixed a couple of switches, that touched either the right or left ear according as we pulled the right or left rein. The ear being the most sensitive part of these animals, the cavesson proved to be as effectual as a bridle and bit.

During the time spent in training our onager, a triple hatching among our fowls made us the possessors of more than forty little chicks, which ran about in every direction piping joyously.

This increase in our poultry, joined with the acquisition of the buffalo and the onager, recalled to my mind a project I had formed some time since for building a substantial stable and fowl-house before the rainy season—which I knew could not be far off—came on in its intensity.

Upon the arched roots of our tree we laid a roof made of bamboos and reeds interlaced with each other, covering it with moss and clay, and finishing it off with a coating of tar. We thus had a solid roof upon which we could walk without fear of falling through. We surrounded it with a neat balustrade, which gave it the appearance of a terrace, and in this way rendered the useful ornamental.

The interior of the hut was divided into several compartments, some serving the purpose of stables and barns, and others being set apart for dairy work and provision stores. We knew it would be necessary to gather in a large stock of the latter, because the rainy season, which is the winter of these tropical seasons, would keep us indoors entirely.

One evening as we were returning from digging potatoes, I proposed to my wife that she and the younger children should drive the cart home to Falcon-nest, while Fritz and Ernest accompanied me to the oak wood, to add to the spoils of the day a supply of acorns. Fritz rode proudly upon the onager. Ernest carried his monkey on his shoulder.

We carried empty sacks with us, intending to fill them and place them on the back of the onager, which had rendered us similar services before, though he flatly refused to assist our donkey in drawing a cart.

When we had reached the middle of the wood, I tied Lightfoot to a tree, and we set to work filling our sacks. Our labour was soon at an end, for the acorns were plentiful and easy to pick up.

Just as we were coming away, the monkey suddenly dashed into a thicket, before which he had been sitting with his ears pricked up; and in another instant we heard the screaming of a bird, accompanied by a furious beating of wings. We judged that a battle was in progress between Master Nip and some denizen of the brush-wood.

Ernest, who was first upon the scene of conflict, advanced with caution, and we soon heard him crying out, "Fritz! Fritz! come here! Here is a nest full of eggs! Come and get them while I hold Nip, who is struggling to get at them! The bird is trying to escape!"

Fritz ran to the bush at the top of his speed, and a few minutes afterwards returned with a fine Canadian heath-fowl, similar to one he had fired at and missed some days before. I helped him to tie the legs of the creature, which, as it appeared to me, would be a very valuable addition to our poultry-yard.

Ernest, who had at last got rid of Nip, brought his hat full of eggs, covered over with leaves similar to those of the iris. In showing them to me he said, "I brought these leaves of which the nest was made because they are so long and thin, and altogether so curious that they will serve to amuse Francis."

Our full sacks were then laid upon the onager in such a manner as to leave room for Fritz, who always rode the animal. Ernest carried his eggs, I the fowl, and in this order we set out for Falcon-nest.

My wife was delighted with our new capture. She carefully laid the eggs in a new nest, induced one of our hens to sit on them, and at the end of twenty days presented us with fifteen young heath-fowls.

A day or two afterwards, when the long sword-like leaves which Ernest had brought home for Francis had become dry, and were blowing about on the grass, Fritz said to his brother, no doubt with the intention of amusing him—"Come on, Francis, let us make some whips of these toys to drive our cattle with!"

Thereupon he proceeded to split each leaf into three or four thongs, which he plaited together into a long cord.

By accident I saw him at work, and noticing the flexibility of the leaves, I examined them more attentively. It gave me intense joy to find that they were leaves of the *Phormium tenax*, a plant which serves the Indians as an admirable substitute for the flax of Europe.

My wife was no less delighted than I was. She cried out enthusiastically, "Bravo! bravo! This is the best discovery we have made yet. Get as many of these leaves as you can, and I will soon make you new clothes of every kind!"

She forgot, the dear creature, how far the raw material in this case was removed from the manufactured article.

While I was endeavouring to explain this to her, with the intention of softening down the disappointment which often follows misplaced enthusiasm, Fritz mounted the onager, Jack the buffalo, and the pair of them disappeared at a gallop in the direction of the oak wood.

In a quarter of an hour they returned, like true foraging hussars, their beasts laden with large bundles of the new flax-plant, which they threw down at our feet.

I commended them for their promptitude, and promised my wife that, whatever might come of our attempt, we would do our best to prepare her some flax.

"First of all," I said, "we must submit our grass to the process of steeping."

"What is steeping?" asked Fritz. "Must we make a fire, and heat some water?"

"No," I replied, "there is no need of a fire. Steeping consists in exposing the flax alternately to moisture and the open air, in order to allow the plant to decay to a certain extent. The soft parts are then easily separated from the long and tenacious threads. The vegetable glue which binds them together is dissolved, and they are obtained by pounding or stripping the stalk."

"But do not the threads perish with the rest?" asked Fritz.

"That may happen," I replied, "if the steeping process lasts too long. At the same time the wonderful toughness of the fibre renders such an accident very rare. Besides, we have nothing to fear if, in place of exposing the grass to the heat of the sun, we carefully put it to decay in stagnant water."

My wife was of opinion that it would be better, owing to the tropical heat of the country in which we found ourselves, to adopt the latter method of steeping, and suggested that Flamingo Marsh would be a good place to carry out the process.

The idea was an excellent one, and next morning we harnessed the ass to the car, upon which we piled our bundles of flax, leaving room for little Francis and Nip in the centre. Thus prepared, we set out, I and the boys following the convoy with our pickaxes and shovels.

Arrived at the marsh, we separated our flax into little bundles, and, tying a stone to each, sunk them in the water till they were entirely submerged.

At the end of fifteen days our good housewife, thinking that the flax was sufficiently steeped, asked us to go and fetch it. We did so, and laid it out on the grass in the sun. In a single day it was quite dry. We then brought it back to Falcon-nest, putting off till another day the pounding and other processes.

As I foresaw the speedy approach of the rainy season, I thought it wise to devote our attention to our stock of edibles.

For some days past the weather, which had hitherto been warm and serene, became at times gloomy and threatening. The heavens were often obscured by thick clouds, the wind moaned up heavy with moisture, and once or twice slight showers had fallen.

All the potatoes and tapioca we could get were brought into the storehouse and piled in heaps; for these roots were to form the staple of our provisions for the winter. We also brought in large supplies of cocoa-nuts and acorns.

In the place of potatoes and tapioca I sowed wheat, for, notwithstanding the many and delicious natural products of the island, we all missed our bread. It is an article of food of which one must be deprived before he can learn the full value of it. Little Francis, who had never cared for bread at home, was more clamorous for it now than any of us.

We took care also to transplant to Undertent a quantity of young cocoa-trees and sugar-canes.

In spite of all our activity and foresight, the rains came upon us before we expected them. They fell in such torrents that little Francis, seriously alarmed for his safety, asked me if there was not going to be another flood, and if we had not better set about building an ark like the patriarch Noah.

We soon found that we could no longer live in our aerial dwelling: the winds and the rain distressed us to the last degree of endurance. So we took up our habitation under the roof which we had thrown over the arched roots of our tree. The chambers, however, were so full of provisions, and animals, and tools, that we had hardly room to move. Nor was this the worst. We could not light a fire without being almost suffocated by smoke.

In order to make room, a large number of articles were piled up the winding staircase, and all our animals were housed in one stall. We were thus enabled to work, and could almost lay ourselves out at full length to sleep. As to cooking, we did as little of it as possible. Our desire for warm food gave way before the terrible ordeal of enduring the smoke which resulted from preparing it.

Besides, we had gathered in but a very limited supply of firewood. So we had every cause for thankfulness when we found that the only effect of the rains upon the atmosphere was to render it humid. Had the winter been cold as well as wet, we should have suffered dreadfully.

Our stock of forage for the animals was not large, and we could not add to it from our own stores of potatoes without being in danger of perishing by hunger ourselves. We therefore decided to give freedom to those of our dumb companions which were indigenous to the country, in order that they might find food for themselves. At the same time, as it was important not to leave them to resume their wild life, Fritz and I, several times during the day and each evening, went to seek them and bring them back to the foot of the tree.

My wife, seeing that we returned each time wet to the skin, hit upon the idea of making each of us a waterproof garment.

To that end she took two sailors' canvas shirts, to which she sewed a kind of hood which we could pull over our heads, and then covered the whole with a coating of caoutchouc. Encased in these garments, we could go out in the heaviest rain without danger to our clothes or to our health.

The captain's chest of books had been opened, and we found them a great relief to us. The box contained some very useful volumes, consisting of dictionaries, scientific works illustrated with cuts, and a great many handbooks for arts and handicrafts. These volumes were not by any means perfect. We often found the authors at fault, especially when they treated of the tropical plants, trees, and animals which had fallen under our own observation.

Of all my labours, that which pleased my wife the most was the making of a card for the purpose of combing our flax.

In order to do so, I rounded and sharpened with a file a number of long nails, which I laid at equal distances one from the other on a square piece of tin. Then I folded the tin over and poured melted lead between the pieces to fix the nails solidly in their places. The next process was to nail the contrivance to a piece of wood, and the flax-comb was complete.

My invention appeared so strong, and so well fitted to its purpose, that my wife prayed for the end of the winter, in order that we might get to flax-carding at once.

CHAPTER 13

*Return of the Fine Season—The Salt Cavern—A Shoal of
Herrings—Salmon—Sturgeons—The Maize-Field*

In towns the winter has its compensations. Comfortable houses,
family reunions around the domestic hearth, pleasant evenings, and
warm beds to lie in, often cause those whom fortune has thus
favoured to forget that the cold season is a time of acute suffering for
the poor. No one, however, is insensible to the advent of the spring
and summer.

As to us, it would be impossible to describe our joy when, after
long weeks of privation and forced seclusion, we at length saw the
skies clear up and the sun shining radiantly upon the glorious face of
nature. It was with transports of delight that we abandoned our
unhealthy dwelling-place to breathe the fresh air again, and to
contemplate the beautiful scenery by which we were surrounded.

Everything seemed to be putting on a new youth. We ourselves felt
inspired by such excellent spirits that we cast far behind us all
remembrance of our past weariness and suffering, and gave our
minds wholly to the labours which lay before us, and which seemed
in our new condition of mind to be little more than pleasant
pastimes.

One of our first cares was to make a tour of inspection over the
enclosed lands which we called our domain.

Our shrubbery was in excellent condition. The seeds which we had
sown were springing up. The new leaves of the trees were budding
forth. The fertile soil was covered with flowers, whose soft odours
were borne upon every passing breeze. The music of birds of the
most brilliant plumage resounded everywhere. We had never hailed
the return of a spring-time so gay and so smiling.

My wife wished to proceed without delay to the carding of our
flax. While, therefore, the younger children were employed in
getting in fresh forage for the animals, Fritz and I spread the
bundles of flax in the sun. When they were sufficiently dry we all
proceeded to the work of pounding, stripping, and carding.

The boys, armed each with a large staff, beat the stalks. My wife, aided by Francis and Ernest, did the stripping. I devoted myself to the carding, and succeeded so well that my impatient wife begged me without delay to make her a spindle, in order that she might turn my rude heaps of flax into thread fit for weaving.

By dint of skill and application—what cannot a willing man accomplish?—I contrived to make, not only a spindle, but a spinning-wheel and a winder.

My wife, transported with zeal, at once set to work without even taking a day's airing, although she had been shut up so many weeks. She consented voluntarily to stay at home with little Francis, while Fritz, Ernest, Jack, and I made an excursion to her favourite Undertent—her sole desire at this time being to provide us with a new supply of clothes to take the place of our old ones, which were fast wearing out.

We found the tent in a deplorable condition. Half of it had been carried away by the wind, and the greater part of our provisions were spoiled by the rain.

We at once took measures to dry everything that we thought could be saved by this means.

Happily our pinnace had suffered no harm. Our tub-boat, on the contrary, was a complete wreck.

The loss which troubled me most was that of two barrels of gunpowder, which, being open, I had left in the tent for current use instead of carrying them to the magazine in the rocks, where, fortunately, I had stored the remaining four barrels.

This accident led me to conceive the project of building substantial winter quarters, where we could find shelter, not only for ourselves, but for our provisions during the heavy tropical rains.

I dared not hope to carry out a bold project of Fritz's, to excavate for ourselves a dwelling in the rocks; for, with such tools and strength as we had at our disposal, I saw that this would be the work of several summers. But I determined, in any case, to try to make a cave large enough to serve as a provision-store.

With this view I set out in the morning, accompanied by Fritz and Jack, who were armed, as I was, with crowbars, pickaxes, and hammers. We chose a place where the face of the rock was even and almost perpendicular to the soil. On this I marked with charcoal the shape of the opening we intended to make; and then we began work vigorously.

We had penetrated to a depth of about seven feet, when Jack, who was working inside the cavity, and was trying with his crowbar to loosen a large piece of rock, suddenly cried out, "I am through! I am through!"

"He is right!" cried Fritz, who had rushed in to see what was going on. "His crowbar has pierced a hole, and fallen through on the other side."

I went in, and was soon convinced of the truth of what Fritz had said. I struck the rock a sharp blow with my pickaxe, and a mass of it fell away, revealing a large opening, into which the boys were about to rush without further thought.

I stopped them instantly, for the air which came out of the hole was foul in the extreme—almost overpowering me when I approached to look in.

I took advantage of the opportunity to teach the boys what were the conditions under which air would sustain life by respiration.

"It is necessary," I said, "that the gases of which air in its normal condition is composed should be in their exact proportions, and not mixed with any other gas emanating from nature. And there are many ways both of discovering whether these proportions have been duly kept, and of avoiding their injurious effects if they have not. The surest test is fire. It not only will not burn except in air which is fit to breathe, but it may be used in one way to drive away the noxious gases from impure air."

We made a first experiment by throwing into the opening some bundles of dry grass which we had set alight. They went out instantly.

I then had recourse to a means which I believed would be more efficacious.

We had saved from the wreck a case of rockets and grenades, such as are used on board ship for giving signals at night. I took some of these, placed them on the edge of the opening, pointing inwards, and then lighted their fuses. The matches hissed for a time, the grenades and rockets exploded, and by the light which they spread abroad we could see the whole interior of the cave. It appeared very deep, and its sides glittered as if they had been cut with as many facets as a diamond.

In an instant all was in darkness again, and nothing was to be seen but the huge waves of thick smoke that floated out of the mouth of the grotto.

When we had fired into the cave two or three times more, I made a second trial with the lighted grass. This time it burnt up brilliantly.

I concluded, therefore, that there was no longer the least danger of asphyxia. Nevertheless, as the cave was in total darkness, and there might be precipices and pools of water in it, I judged it prudent not to enter without a light.

I dispatched Jack to Falcon-nest to announce our happy discovery to the other members of the family, to get them to come along with him and assist in the work of exploration, and also to bring enough candles to examine the cave throughout its extent.

While Jack was away, Fritz and I enlarged the entrance to our grotto, and cleared away the rubbish that lay before it.

We had just finished when we saw our good housewife and the three younger boys approaching, mounted upon our chariot, of which Jack had constituted himself the noisy driver. Ernest and Francis waved their hats as a sign of triumph.

We entered altogether into the cavern, each of us carrying a lighted candle. Fritz and I took a tinder-box each, lest any of the candles should go out.

Our expedition had an air of gravity, if not of solemnity, about it. I led the way myself, cautiously sounding the earth, and looking round on every hand as I went. My boys, spurred on by curiosity, followed me courageously.

The floor of the cavern, which a providential hand seemed thus to have prepared for our reception, was solid and level, and covered with a very fine, dry sand.

Having examined the disposition of the crystals in a piece of stone which I chipped off the side of the cavern, and placed the fragment to my lips, I found that the grotto was formed in a vein of rock-salt.

This discovery gave me the liveliest satisfaction, for it assured us of a plentiful supply of salt both for ourselves and our animals, without the labour of gathering it as we had hitherto done upon the sea-shore.

Some steps further on, I came upon some pieces of crystal which seemed to have fallen from the roof.

This discovery led us to fear that these droppings might be continual, in which case it would be dangerous to inhabit the cave; but seeing no more about, I came to the conclusion that our explosions had loosened these fragments, and that in ordinary circumstances the roof was perfectly safe.

Nevertheless, to make quite sure, I sent everybody out of the cavern, and fired off a gun two or three times into the mouth of it. A few more pieces fell; but on sounding the roof with a pole, we found that these pieces were only exceptions, and that, as a whole, the top of the grotto was as solid as its sides.

When we had finally decided to take up our winter quarters in the cavern, no one knows the projects that were conceived for fitting it up.

Falcon-nest was to remain as a summer residence, but we thought no more of the improvements we had resolved to make there to fit it for the rainy season. Our attention was wholly concentrated upon our subterranean house. In the first place we carved out a handsome doorway, and in the next, we made apertures in the face of the rock. To these openings we fitted the doors and windows of the tree at Falcon-nest; for, since the latter was henceforth to be only a summer residence, there was no need of closing it up so carefully.

The cavern being very large, we divided it into separate apartments by partitions. To the right of the entrance were placed our sitting and sleeping rooms; to the left, the kitchen and the workshop. Further back were placed our cellar and store-room. We had four apartments in that side of the cave which we had set apart for habitation. The first was intended as a sleeping apartment for my wife and myself; the second was the dining-room; then came a bedroom for the boys; and behind this was a large sitting-room, where we placed the books, the arms, and certain curiosities that we had collected from the wreck during our sojourn on the island.

In the room intended for the kitchen we constructed a large fireplace, with a chimney passing out at the top of the rock in which the cave was situated.

All our provisions and tools had places of their own; but, notwithstanding the enormous extent of the cavern, the greatest ingenuity was requisite to find room for our poultry and animals. Never since we had been on the island had we displayed so much skill and activity. At the same time we were continually stimulated to fresh labours by the satisfactory results we achieved.

While we were employed in fitting up our grotto residence, we were obliged to take up our habitation at Undertent, and our food consisted chiefly of turtles' eggs and the flesh of a turtle or two which we caught as they came up on the beach to lay. It occurred to me that it would not be at all a bad thing to keep turtles, so that we could provide ourselves according to our needs, without the trouble of waiting to capture them. I also hit upon a plan for carrying out my idea. Whenever we saw a turtle on the beach, Fritz ran out and cut off its retreat to the sea while we caught it and turned it over upon its back. Then with a drill we bored a hole in the edge of its shell, through which we passed a long cord that we fastened to a stake. The turtle was thus at liberty to plunge into the sea again or to walk about on land as much as he pleased; but he was not the less our prisoner, and we could make use of him when we wanted him.

One morning as we were making our way from Falcon-nest to Deliverance Bay, we were arrested by a strange sight out at sea. About a thousand paces from the shore, a vast extent of water seemed to be boiling, and sparkled vividly in the morning sun. Just over this brilliant wave-mass sailed a great cloud of sea-mews and others birds, which were screaming loudly.

It became evident that we were witnessing the arrival of a shoal of herrings.

Fritz went into the sea with a basket, which it was only necessary to submerge in order to fill it with fish. I threw the herrings upon the sand. Francis picked them up and carried them to Ernest and Jack, who, with the help of their knives, disembowelled them in accordance with a method which I described. This done, I fetched the remaining casks of our old tub-boat, and placed the herrings in them in layers, between each of which my wife scattered a good sprinkling of salt. When I had in this way filled all the casks, I closed them with some pieces of board, which I nailed down securely; and then, with the help of our donkey and cart, we transported our spoils to the new store-house in the grotto.

About a month after we were visited by the shoal of herrings, Jackal River was invaded by a quantity of salmon and sturgeon, which came up the stream, as their custom is, to spawn in fresh water.

Jack, who was the first to notice these new visitors, took them for young whales.

I had no difficulty in pointing out to him his error; and I cast about for some means of capturing a few of these fish, of which the flesh is very delicate eating.

Jack, who remarked, or rather, perhaps, divined the nature of my reflections, darted off at full speed, crying, "Wait a moment, papa! wait a moment! I think I know of a plan for catching sturgeon and salmon."

It was not long before he returned, carrying a bow, some arrows with barbed points, a ball of stout string, and two or three bladders which we had taken out of dog-fish.

Curious to see what he was going to do with these implements, his mother, his brothers, and I went with him to the bank of the river.

Arrived there, he tied a piece of string round one of the bladders, and then fastened it to an arrow. The other end of the string he made fast to a huge stone at the water's edge. Then, drawing his bow, he sighted a huge salmon. The arrow sped swiftly on its mission, and buried itself in the side of the fish.

"A hit! a hit!" cried the young archer, dancing with delight.

The salmon darted off like a flash of lightning, but soon found itself pulled up by the weight of the stone and the air in the bladder. The injury caused by so sudden a stoppage, joined with the rankling of the iron in his flesh, soon wore him out, and we were able to draw him to the bank without much difficulty.

Jack's ingenuity and success drove us all to emulation. Fritz went to seek the harpoon and windlass. I armed myself, like the god Neptune, with a trident. Ernest furnished himself with fish-hooks, which he baited with pieces of the first salmon caught. Salmon-fishing in every fashion began in earnest.

Jack held to the method which had already stood him in such good stead. He discharged two or three arrows without hitting his mark, and when he did strike home, it was not without great difficulty that he landed his new victim.

Ernest got a bite from a sturgeon, which, with the aid of little Francis and his mother, he managed to pull out.

As to Fritz, he economised his labour. He refrained from throwing his harpoon till he saw passing within range a sturgeon which measured at least ten feet in length. Struck full in the back, the enormous creature struggled fiercely, leaping and making the water fly in every direction. We were obliged to let out all the rope in the windlass to prevent our important catch from escaping. Then, little by little, we drew him into the shallows. Even then, however, we were obliged to go into the water and slip a noose over his gills before we could drag him to land.

The morning's sport at an end, we cleaned our fish, and put aside the roe of the sturgeon and the bladders for a particular use to which I designed to put them. The greater part of the flesh, after being cut in slices, was salted after the same manner as the herrings.

I determined to cure the rest in the same fashion as they cure the tunny-fish on the coasts of the Mediterranean. For this purpose I had some water boiled and strongly salted, which I poured into a tub containing the slices of fish, together with a small quantity of oil.

My wife, thinking not that the roes and bladders were of any use, was about to throw them into the water, when I stopped her, observing that I intended to prepare from the roes a very choice dish which the Russians called "caviare", and from the bladders a valuable gelatinous substance called "fish-glue".

Without further delay, I carefully washed the roes, which in the mass weighed about thirty pounds. We then laid them to soak in salt water for several hours. It now only remained to press them into our calabash sieves, where the water was all drained off, to obtain a dozen hard and compact cakes of caviare, which were afterwards smoked in our curing-hut. Our stock of provisions for the winter was thus augmented by a delicacy for which kings have sometimes sighed in vain.

I recollected to have read or heard tell of the process whereby fish-glue was prepared, and I resolved to put it in practice. I cut the bladders into strips, which I first laid in water to soften them, and then in the sun to dry them. We thus obtained a kind of shavings which, thrown into boiling water, would dissolve and yield a very pure gelatine. This gelatine, poured upon a flat surface, formed in cooling a highly-transparent film, which I hoped would serve to glaze our windows.

The garden at Undertent was remarkably fertile, and yielded, almost without culture, excellent vegetables of every kind. We had only to water it to bring forth its products in rich abundance; and even this operation gave us very little trouble, for by this time we had laid down the two halves of the sago-palm, and a plentiful supply of water was thus brought upon the ground from Jackal River.

The greater part of the plants were perfectly acclimatised already. The trailing stalks of the melons and cucumbers were loaded with fruit; the bananas gave rich promise of future treasures; the maize showed ripening ears everywhere. Judging by the condition of the garden close to our home, it augured well of those further removed from us. In the morning we set out in a body to visit them.

On the road to Falcon-nest we made a halt in the old potato-field, which my wife had sown with all kinds of seeds after gathering in her harvest of tubers. There also we were met by marvels in vegetation. Barley, peas, lentils, millet, oats, and several other cereals were growing in abundance.

I wondered where my wife had managed to find enough seed to sow so large a piece of land; and I was especially struck with a part of the field which was covered with a tall and thick growth of maize, come to full maturity. The richness of the vegetation had, no doubt, brought a great many destructive parasites to the spot: we could see their traces everywhere. As we approached the maize-field to cut some of it for present use, we disturbed a halfdozen bustards, which flew off with a great beating of wings; while a large number of smaller birds, amongst which I recognised the quail, ran away as fast as their legs could carry them. Two or three kangaroos also went hopping away, and our dogs followed them, but without being able to make a capture.

Fritz, who had his eagle with him, put it up, and it pounced skilfully upon one of the bustards, which it brought down, merely wounding and not killing it, however, so that we were able to add it to our other poultry.

Jack's jackal, which began by this time to be a keen hunter, brought in something like a dozen quails, which were very fat, and furnished us with an excellent repast.

We now resumed our journey, and by the middle of the afternoon found ourselves once more at Falcon-nest. As the heat of the day and our long walk had made us very thirsty, my wife proposed to prepare us a new beverage. Bruising some grains of the maize, which were still very soft, she squeezed them in a cloth, and obtained a thick liquid, which she diluted with water and sweetened with the juice of some sugar-canes. This done, she presented each of us with a cup of milky liquor, as pleasant to the taste as it was refreshing.

The remainder of the day was employed in removing our maize from the husk, and in making preparations for the execution of a project which I had conceived some time before. My idea was to establish in the open country a sort of colony of animals, which, if they acclimatised themselves and propagated their species, would relieve us of the troublesome task of tending and feeding them. I felt that there was no great danger in making the attempt, for by this time our barn-yard was so full of poultry and other livestock that we could risk the sacrifice of at least one of each species without feeling the loss of them.

CHAPTER 14

The Cotton Plant—Forest Grange—The Pirogue—Francis' Charge

The next morning, then, at daybreak we set out, having previously loaded our car—in addition to a supply of provisions—with ten fowls, two cocks, three young pigs, and two pairs of goats. The cow, the buffalo, and the ass were yoked to it. Fritz, mounted on the onager, went on some distance in front of the caravan to reconnoitre.

Our course was directed towards a point of our domains which we had not yet explored—that is to say, towards the region which extended from Falcon-nest to the large bay beyond Cape Disappointment.

At the outset of the journey we had frequently to open a road with our hatchets, for we traversed fields obstructed with high grass and thickets; but soon the caravan reached a small wood, on leaving which we saw before us a plateau covered with shrubs, which appeared to be loaded with white flakes.

"Snow! snow!" cried Francis joyously, and he jumped up from the bottom of the carriage, where he was sitting. "Here is a country where they have winters of the right sort. It is not like Falcon-nest, where it does nothing but rain half the year."

And repeating "Snow! snow!" he ran forward quickly with the intention of making a snowball.

We all laughed at the simplicity of his remarks.

It was not long before I got an insight into the nature of the supposed snow. "Well," said I to our young scholar, who was still greatly amused at his brother's mistake, "do you know the name of these shrubs?"

"As far as I can judge," he replied, with a certain air of importance, "they are the cotton-plant; and if it should prove so, it will be easy to make an ample provision of cotton without much trouble."

He was right. The field presented a very curious spectacle. The pods of the plants, arrived at maturity, had burst, allowing the escape of the down with which they were filled. Part of it still fluttered on the branches of the shrubs. A large quantity had been stripped off by the wind, and lay scattered about, whitening all the ground.

This discovery was a source of much rejoicing to us all. My wife was particularly delighted. She immediately asked me if it would not be possible for us to construct a weaving-loom, for she already foresaw a means of renewing our stock of linen, which was much worn.

I promised her that I would think of some method of meeting her wishes.

Meanwhile we made a point of filling those of our sacks which were empty with the cotton. My wife collected also a quantity of the seeds of the plant, which she proposed to sow in the vicinity of Undertent, with the view of obtaining a supply of cotton nearer home.

Our harvest finished, we continued our journey. Soon we reached a small hill, from the top of which we obtained a magnificent view. The sides of it were covered with the most gorgeous vegetation. At the foot of it was the plain that we proposed to traverse, fertilised by a large river.

A tent was soon erected. A fire was made, and our good housewife, assisted by Francis and Jack, occupied herself in preparing a repast.

I remarked a group of trees placed so conveniently each with regard to the other, that I resolved on making them serve as the pillars of the farmery which we proposed to construct.

Our plans completed for the next day's work, we returned to the tent, where an excellent supper awaited us.

My wife distributed the cotton we had collected into bundles, so that we all had comfortable pillows for our heads; and we enjoyed our slumbers that night more than we had done for a long time past.

The trees which I had chosen for the construction of the hut were six in number, and formed an oblong, one side of which faced the sea.

In the trunks of the first three—I thus designated those which were nearest the shore—I cut, at about a dozen feet from the ground, some notches, into which I fixed a strong pole. I then repeated the process with the trunks of the other three trees—here, however, fixing my pole at a height of only eight feet. I then laid a row of smaller poles from the higher to the lower level, to form a roof, which I covered with strips of bark, to supply the place of tiles.

With wild vines and flexible reeds, woven strongly together, I then built up four outer walls to the height of five feet. In the open space between the top of these and the roof I placed some trellis-work, which allowed the air and light to penetrate to the interior.

The door was made facing the sea, in what we intended to be the front of the building. The inside was so fitted as best to meet the end we had in view, with the least expenditure of wood.

A partition, raised to half the height of the building, separated it into two unequal divisions, the largest of which was intended for the sheepfold. I set apart here a place for the fowls, shutting it off from the rest of the compartment by a palisade, the bars of which, while allowing free ingress and egress for the feathered tribe, were too close together to permit of the passage of larger animals.

A door led from the sheepfold into the other part of the cabin, which we fitted up as a temporary lodging-place for ourselves.

All this had been done very quickly, and by consequence somewhat roughly; but I promised myself to endeavour to improve matters when we had a little spare time. For the present it sufficed that our livestock had a place of shelter.

In order to accustom them to return in the evening to their stable, the troughs were filled with grain and mixed with salt, and it was agreed that this enticement should be renewed until our winged and four-footed colonists were habituated to their new dwelling.

The next day, after having supplied with an abundant provision of food the livestock which we left behind, we quitted the farmery, to which we had given the name of Forest Grange.

In the first wood which we passed through on our route we encountered a troop of monkeys, that welcomed us with the most horrible screams, accompanied by a shower of fir-cones. I fired into the air several times, in order that we might be relieved of their embarrassing attentions. On examining some of the cones which they had thrown at us, I found they had a very agreeable taste, and were of a kind that would yield an excellent oil. I recommended the youngsters to make an abundant provision of them. We then resumed our journey, and were not long in arriving at Cape Disappointment, on which I had resolved to put up a hut, which should serve us as a fishing-place when we made excursions along the coast.

We set vigorously to work. Our experience at Forest Grange had given us the skill which comes with practice; and in less than a week we finished the building, which was honoured by our young scholar with the name of "Prospect Hill".

For some time I had been on the look-out for a tree, the bark of which I had read would make a canoe, combining strength and lightness; and although my search had been so far fruitless, I had not lost all hope of succeeding in my object.

As soon as the hut was finished, my boys and I explored the surrounding neighbourhood, which abounded in rare trees. We found several that we should have deemed oaks by their height and foliage, had not their fruit, although much resembling acorns, shown us otherwise by their extreme smallness.

After having chosen one that seemed to me most suitable for the object we had in view, Fritz and I attached to the lower branches of it the rope-ladder which we had brought with us from Falcon-nest. Mounted upon this, Fritz proceeded to saw through the bark at the top of the trunk until he came to the wood, while I performed a similar operation at the base. I then stripped off a narrow riband of bark, extending from the one incision to the other, and by means of wooden wedges, cautiously forced into the opening, separated the rest of the covering in one solid piece. As the tree was full of sap, and the bark consequently very flexible, that portion of our task was perfectly successful; but the most difficult part still remained to be performed, and that was to convert the spoil into a pirogue or savage's canoe.

While the bark was yet moist and supple, I gave it the shape required. I cut with my hatchet a slit in the two ends, lapped the parts thus separated over each other, and nailed them together again in such a manner that they formed a point at each extremity. We had thus advanced one stage in the work of shaping our contrivance for easy navigation. Still, the pirogue was entirely flat in the middle; so I had recourse to ropes, and by a judicious tying down here and bracing up there, managed to get the sides of the boat into something like their proper shape.

But as I could not finish my task without the assistance of my tools, I sent Fritz and Jack to the tent to bring the truck, to which I had fixed the wheels of a cannon found aboard the wreck, proposing to place the pirogue on it and transport it to a more convenient spot, in order to finish it.

While waiting for their return, Ernest and I made an excursion into our immediate neighbourhood, where we found a certain tree called Fire-wood by the Indians, and which they employ when requiring a light for their nocturnal expeditions. I cut, on our journey, some pieces of wood of a shape that would serve for the ribs of the pirogue. We also discovered at the same time a new resin which, when dry, was firm and impervious to water, and remembering that it would be far preferable both to the gums we had and also to turpentine for coating our pirogue, we collected a quantity of it.

Fritz and Jack did not rejoin us until darkness had begun to set in; and as it was then too late to commence operations, we put off work till the morrow.

The first thing in the morning we placed our canoe on the car, together with the pieces of wood and other things which we thought might prove useful to us, and set out for Undertent. We stopped at Falcon-nest about two hours, which gave us sufficient time to dine and feed our animals.

We reached the tent some time before sunset, but were too tired to do anything that evening. The whole of the next day was employed in finishing the boat. In order to strengthen it, I nailed a piece of curved wood to each end, and furnished it with a solid keel running its whole length. Along the top we placed a ledge of flexible laths and poles, furnished with rings, through which to pass the cordage belonging to the mast.

I threw into the bottom as ballast some stones and clay, and covered it over with a floor, upon which we could stand and walk about comfortably. Movable seats were placed across. Our mast, furnished with a triangular sail, was placed in the middle. A rudder was fixed astern.

A happy idea occurred to me, whereby our little craft could be rendered more buoyant. I got my wife to make some air-tight bags from the skin of the dog-fish. These I filled with air, and after having given them a coat of varnish, I fastened them to the outside of the bulwarks. These air-bladders not only aided us in launching our vessel, but also prevented it from being capsized and submerged.

I have omitted to mention in its proper place the fact of our cow having presented us with a male calf, a little while after the rainy season. This animal was already grown to a size which I thought could be turned to account; and so one evening, when we were all assembled, I called Francis to my side.

"Come, little man," I said, "what do you say to undertaking the education of the calf?"

"The very thing, father!" cried he, clapping his hands. "The calf is a gentle creature; I will be kind to him, and give him everything that he likes; and although I am young I shall succeed in the end. First and foremost, I will call my pupil 'Grumbler'; for before his education is finished, I have no doubt he will give vent to many growls and murmurs."

The name was considered appropriate by the boys, who straightway set to work to find names for the buffalo and the two puppies. Jack proposed to call the buffalo "Storm"; for it would be a fine thing, in his view, to hear his brothers cry out when he approached, "Here comes Jack, riding on the 'Storm'!" The dogs were called, the one "Brown" and the other "Fawn", in accordance with their respective colours.

During two whole months we were employed in putting up partitions to separate the cavern into compartments, in order to render our habitation as agreeable as possible; the embellishment and finishing off our work we reserved for the winter.

The great quantity of beams, planks, and other materials which we possessed, rendered our work less difficult than we had at first imagined.

The floor of our chamber was covered by a thick bed of clay, over which was placed a quantity of small pebbles, laid closely and evenly together. The plaster with which we had covered our walls, I calculated, would be properly dried by the end of the summer. The idea occurred to us to utilise the hair of our goats and the wool of our sheep in the fabrication of carpets for the floors of our dining and sitting-rooms. In order to do this, we placed on a piece of sail-cloth a layer of hair, which we had previously carded and which I wetted with fish-glue melted in boiling water. I then rolled up the cloth, and we set to belabouring it with all our might with large sticks. The operation with the glue was again gone through, as was also the beating, which was this time long and vigorous. We then unrolled the sail-cloth, and removed from it a long strip of felt, which, when dried in the sun, answered perfectly the object we had in view. Our carpets were not Turkish ones, but they had their merit for us.

CHAPTER 15

Preparations for the Winter—Divers Labours—The Rains Again

As the rainy season was again approaching, it now became necessary to lay in an abundant stock of provisions and forage, and to take measure for preserving our animals.

I also took means to lay in a supply of fresh water to our winter quarters, of which we had just finished the interior arrangements.

To this end we made a long conduit with hollow bamboo-canes, which we spliced together, and made watertight at the joints with resin. The conduit was much longer than it would otherwise have been, for by the fortifications and hedges with which we had surrounded our dwelling we had completely cut off all access to the nearest point of Jackal River, and had therefore to obtain our supply of water higher up the stream.

One pipe, which was laid upon a long row of forked sticks, emptied itself into a large cask; and when this cask was full, we corked the conduit till we required a fresh supply.

Day by day we devoted ourselves to getting in potatoes, rice, maize, acorns, and every variety of useful plant that we could think of. The savoury anana, you may be sure, was not forgotten.

As we had not vessels enough to hold all our spoils, my wife made us some sacks out of the remains of the sail-cloth, and we even broke up our raft for the sake of the tubs of which it was made.

In the midst of all our labours, I had not forgotten that our farmery had to be made safe from the monkeys.

"How would it be if we were to put some little windmill sails at each corner of the hut? Would not that keep the monkeys away?" asked Jack.

We all set to work at once, and a few hours afterwards as many as thirty miniature windmills were spinning away all over the estate.

Before long the storms set in, and the fine weather was at an end.

Thunder, lightning, and driving rain compelled us to take refuge in our grotto. The sea took part in the general convulsion of nature, and the noise of the waves as they roared in-shore and burst booming upon the rocks filled us at first with an involuntary and indescribable terror.

I had not expected these storms till the month of June, but they came upon us long before that; and we were obliged to remain confined for twelve weeks to our winter quarters.

We only kept four of our animals in the stable at the grotto—the cow to provide us with milk, the onager to feed its little one, and the buffalo and the donkey to carry us to Falcon-nest from time to time to look after our poultry, feed our animals, and bring back supplies of forage to the cavern.

It is hardly necessary to say that we also kept near us the dogs, the eagle, the jackal, and the monkey, whose antics diverted us amazingly.

With our spare timber, and some pieces of rock taken from the cavern, we laid a terrace along the front of our new abode, and thereupon erected a bamboo verandah surmounted by a balcony, from which we could survey the surrounding country.

We soon found that the fitting-up of the cavern, although it had been the object of all our cares, was in no sense complete. The three openings in the rock which served for windows, for instance, admitted but a feeble light into the interior. It is true we determined to remedy this defect thoroughly when the rains were over, but it was necessary to do something immediately, for it was by no means pleasant to remain buried in the dark for weeks together.

I took a long and thick bamboo, one end of which I solidly fixed in the floor of the cavern, while the other touched the vaulted roof.

Jack climbed up this pole, and with a hammer drove securely into a natural crevice in the rock a stout wooden stake, upon which was fixed a pulley whose ropes reached to the ground.

While he was thus engaged, his mother cleaned and trimmed with oil a lantern which he had found on the wreck. We then lighted its three wicks, fastened it to the ropes of the pulley, and drew it up to a convenient height. The crystal facets of the vaulted roof flung back its light in a thousand sparkling forms.

The arrangement of the different apartments occupied us several days. Ernest and Francis put up shelves for the books. My wife and Jack fitted up the sitting-room and the kitchen. Fritz and I reserved to ourselves the arrangement of the workshop, as that involved the heaviest labour.

In this apartment we placed the captain's lathe, the carpenter's bench and tool-chest, and all the cooper's and gunsmith's tools that we had brought away from the wreck.

In one corner we fitted up a forge. We had a pair of bellows, an anvil, and some hammers; but we required a great many more tools than we had to enable us to set up the trade of blacksmith.

Thanks to the industry of our young scholar and Jack, the library soon began to look quite like a museum. Upon the shelves were ranged the books which had belonged to the captain and officers of the ship. They consisted of works of natural history illustrated with coloured engravings, treatises on botany and zoology, and other works not less useful. To these were added an excellent supply of mathematical and astronomical instruments, and a large terrestrial globe. Beside these, again, were ranged the natural history specimens which we had collected since our sojourn on the island.

Among the educational books we found several grammars and dictionaries of different languages. We determined to make use of these to perfect our knowledge in the tongues of which we knew so little, and to learn others of which we knew nothing: so that we might be able to converse with the sailors of any ship that might chance to call, if God so willed it, at our island. We knew French well. Our mother tongue was German. Fritz and Ernest proposed to learn English. Jack decided in favour of Italian and Spanish, which seemed to him to sound more pompously on the ear.

Ernest made up his mind to learn Latin also, a very useful language in the study of natural history and medicine, of which we had several treatises in our library.

Furthermore, he took upon himself the duty of instructing his brother Francis, who progressed so well that, far from being frightened at books, as was formerly the case, he awaited with impatience the hour at which he was in the habit of receiving his lessons.

For myself, I resolved to learn the Malay language, thinking it not impossible that we might some day be favoured with a visit from some Indians of an adjacent island or mainland.

CHAPTER 16

The Dead Whale

At length the weather changed. The sky became blue, and we were able to leave our retreat to breathe the fresh air again.

While we were engaged in contemplating the phenomena of the new vegetation that surrounded us, the lynx-eyed Fritz saw something lying near a small island in an inlet of the bay, which looked like a capsized boat. I took the telescope, but could not make out at all clearly what it was.

We thereupon determined to make an excursion across the intervening island in order to get a nearer view of it. Besides, we had need of air and exercise after our three months' seclusion.

Having emptied our pirogue of the rain-water with which it was filled and furnished it with its rigging, we set out—Fritz, Ernest, Jack, and I.

As we came nearer to the object of our journey, our first conjecture vanished, and we soon saw that what we had fancied to be an overturned canoe was neither more nor less than a huge whale, which the violence of the sea had flung upon a jutting point of the island. The waves, which beat furiously upon the coast where the whale lay, forced us to make a detour to get to land.

I quickened my steps, and soon overtook the boys, who had walked round the beach. They showed me their caps, filled with coral and seashells, which they had picked up on the way, and concerning which they overwhelmed me with questions.

The boys, who found working at the oars a somewhat laborious occupation, asked me if I did not think I could invent some contrivance whereby the pirogue might be made to glide over the waves without so much effort on our parts.

I smiled as I thought of the unlimited confidence they placed in my ingenuity.

"I am not a sorcerer," I said, "nor have I a fairy always at my elbow. Nevertheless, if you will undertake to find me a large iron wheel, I will at least promise to do the best I can to meet your wishes."

"An iron wheel!" cried Fritz. "Why, there is a capital one on one of our roasting spits!"

On the following day we furnished our pirogue with tools and provisions, and also put on board a few tubs. We then embarked and weighed anchor. The sea was calm, and we had no difficulty in landing close to the whale, whose size and hideous aspect frightened Francis and his mother not a little. It was, indeed, an enormous beast, measuring not less than seventy feet in length, and weighing several tons. It was as ugly as it was large. My children were overcome with fear as they reflected upon the fate that would have befallen us had we met such a creature as this during any of our voyages to the vessel.

We set to work at once to cut the monster up.

We did not carry on our offensive but useful labours alone. A multitude of birds of prey, undaunted by our presence, settled upon the carcase, and carried their effrontery to the point of flying away with the slices which we cut off with our knives. The boys killed several of them, and as our good housewife said she should be glad to have their feathers, we put them in our boat.

We filled our tubs with pieces of blubber cut off the flanks of the whale, and with our precious cargo—of which, however, the odour was not very agreeable—we returned to Rock-house.

The next morning I announced a new plan of procedure, but my wife and little Francis declined to be of the party, the work we proposed to do being repugnant to them. I had determined to open the body of the animal.

Before beginning work we took off our ordinary garments, and dressed ourselves in some rough ones which my wife had prepared for the purpose.

Fritz and I then opened the body of the monster with our hatchets, and drew hence the liver, the sinews of the tail, and lastly the entrails, of which I intended to make bags to hold the oil which we extracted from the blubber. This task achieved, we hastened to set out for land again.

My wife regarded our odorous spoils with no great pleasure. I softened her a little by promising that, however unpleasant our cargo might be at present, I should extract from it unheard-of treasures.

The next morning at daybreak we proceeded to convert our blubber into oil.

After having, by heavy pressure, obtained a first running of fine, pure oil, with which we filled two of our tubs, we fed our cauldron several times with pieces of flesh, and, with the assistance of a brisk fire, obtained ten large skinfuls of ordinary train-oil.

Although we took care to perform this operation at some distance from Rock-house, the insupportable smell which exhaled from the cauldron failed not to penetrate even to the inner chambers.

"Why on earth," asked my wife, when we assembled at dinner, "did you not carry on this abominable manufacture on the island? You would have found enough wood there to melt down a hundred times as much oil, and we should not have been poisoned by the stench. While on the point, too, I may as well tell you of an idea that has occurred to me. Why cannot we establish a colony of poultry on this same island? There, at least, there would be nothing to fear either from jackals or monkeys."

"A capital notion!" cried I. "We will endeavour to carry it out as soon as possible."

CHAPTER 17

The Loom Finished—The Palanquin—The Boa

It was at this time that, with the assistance of Ernest, I finished the loom which I had so long intended to present to our good housewife, who was growing more and more anxious as she saw our stock of linen decreasing daily without any apparent means of replacing it.

My success encouraged me. I resolved to try my hand at the manufacture of saddles and harness for the beasts which my boys rode.

The saddles were already cut out, and I re-covered them with kangaroo's skin and stuffed them with moss. I also made straps, bridles, traces, and other articles; but as the trade was quite new to me, I found it necessary to do as the tailors do, measure my customers by fitting their new garments on from time to time during the process of manufacture.

I had scarcely finished these labours when we were visited, as in the preceding year, by a shoal of herrings, of which we laid in a plentiful supply.

To the herrings succeeded the dog-fish, of which we killed a score or so, and pickled their skins with salt for future use. The fat and the bladders were carefully put on one side. As to the flesh, we cut it up and threw it into Jackal River for the crabs, of which, thanks to this bait, we took a large quantity, to replenish our exhausted store in the dam we had made for their reception twelve months before.

These fisheries at an end, I determined to see what I could do at making baskets, of which my wife had great need for carrying her seeds and vegetables to and from the garden, and for other purposes.

Our first attempts were made with the common osier, and we took to the work fairly; for although our first productions were rough and unshapely, they did well enough to carry dirt in, and with practice we soon acquired greater skill. Two large baskets that we made were of such excellent form and finish, that Jack and Ernest, proud of their share in the work, put Francis into one of them, and, thrusting a couple of poles through the handles, carried him upon their shoulders in triumph.

"Oh, father!" cried Fritz, all at once, looking and laughing at them for some time, "could we not make a similar litter for mamma? She would find it so much easier than riding on the truck when she accompanies us on our excursions!"

"No doubt, my good Fritz," I replied, "but where are the porters with shoulders strong enough to carry this new palanquin?"

"Have Storm and Grumbler!" cried Jack, putting down Francis, and joining in the conversation. "We can easily harness them, one on the left and the other on the right, to the two poles which support the basket. May we try, father?"

I consented willingly, and the two animals were at once led out.

We put on their saddles, to which we securely fastened the poles that were to support the basket.

Then Jack mounted upon Storm, and Francis upon Grumbler. The beasts knelt at the command of their masters while Ernest got into the basket, and at a second command they got up and walked leisurely away with their load between them.

The palanquin swung as easily and pleasantly as a carriage upon light springs. Little by little, however, the two burly porters quickened their pace, and though this delighted Ernest at first, he soon became so alarmed that he shut his eyes and laid hold of the sides of the basket. Thereupon Jack and Francis, who had remarked the growing fear of their brother and were much amused at it, began whipping their beasts furiously, and they started off at full gallop.

Poor Ernest, tossed hither and thither and jolted up and down, bounded from one side of the basket to the other like an Indiarubber ball, and cried out with all his might to be put down.

The two animals, however, seemed to enjoy the fun as much as their giddy-witted riders, and, after making a wide detour upon the beach at Undertent, brought themselves upon their knees in front of us, as if begging for our applause.

As my wife and I sat quietly conversing in front of the grotto, I noticed that Fritz, who was some paces off, was looking intently towards the avenue which led from the bridge crossing the river to Falcon-nest.

In a moment or two he came up and said, "There is a strange animal of some kind down below there, father. I don't know what it is, but it seems to be coming this way, if one may judge from the movements of the clouds of dust which it raises."

"It is no doubt one of our own animals rolling in the sand," said his mother.

"No, it can't be that," returned Fritz; "all our animals are shut up for the night. Besides, this one, so far as I can make out, is altogether different in form. It looks like a huge cable, now unrolling itself on the ground, now rising erect and swaying from side to side."

At these words my wife, in great alarm, re-entered the grotto, and I sent my boys in after her to get the arms ready.

I then took the telescope and directed it towards the bridge.

An exclamation of horror escaped me.

"What is it, father?" asked Fritz anxiously.

"It is an enormous serpent," I replied in a low voice.

"Then I won't be the last at the fight," cried the courageous boy. "I will go and fetch the guns and the axes."

"Prudence before all," I exclaimed. "This animal is too terrible for us to venture to fight face to face with him."

In saying these words I drew Fritz after me into the grotto, when we set to work preparing to receive the monster.

Our terror was too well grounded. We could distinctly see the fearful reptile trailing his enormous folds along the bank of the river. As soon as he had crossed the bridge, he stopped from time to time, raising his hideous head and surveying his surroundings, as if he were upon new ground and uncertain of his way.

We barricaded the door and stopped up all the openings but one, where we could see without being seen. There, gun in hand, and ears and eyes on the alert, we watched every movement of the approaching enemy.

It was a boa of the very largest size.

The monster made straight towards the grotto. But all at once he seemed to hesitate, as if troubled by the evident traces of human beings.

At this moment Ernest, overcome by excitement, dropped the trigger of his gun, and the piece went off. Jack and Francis, thinking the time had come for action, did the same.

At this triple discharge the serpent raised his head rather in surprise than fright. It may have been that neither shot reached its mark; it may have been that the scales of the creature were impervious to bullets; at any rate he seemed to have received no wound.

Just as Fritz and I, taking careful aim, were about to fire in our turn, the monster glided swiftly away towards Goose Marsh, where he disappeared.

The presence of the boa in the neighbourhood disquieted me not a little. At any moment the terrible animal might reappear, and I knew of no means of getting rid of it without risking a great deal of danger.

During three whole days fear held us prisoners in the grotto. The least noise outside put us in mortal terror. We dared scarcely venture over the threshold.

However, the monster gave no sign of his presence, and we should probably have come to the conclusion that he had left the neighbourhood, had it not been for the way in which our poultry and pigeons cackled and flew from rock to rock, as if they feared the attack of some terrible enemy.

Our anxiety increased hourly while the obstinate refusal of the serpent to show himself only left us the more time to reflect upon the horrors of our situation. On the other hand, our stock of provisions was diminishing rapidly without our being able to renew them, and all our projected employments were suffering from our enforced inaction.

The forage was coming to an end; and we foresaw that the time would shortly arrive when our own food would fail, if we continued to divide with our animals the slender supply of provisions that remained to us.

I determined, therefore, to set the beasts at liberty, in order that they might find fodder for themselves.

We decided to drive them up towards the source of the river in the opposite direction to the marsh, where we concluded the boa still lay concealed.

Fritz took this hazardous duty upon himself.

He drove the beasts out, and was making ready to escort them, while the rest of us stood at the window with our loaded guns, in readiness to fire should he be interrupted in his work. The buffalo and the cow were already yoked together, when the ass, to whom three days' rest and an abundancy of good food had imparted an extraordinary amount of vigour and playfulness, dashed off into the open ground, he-hawing so loudly and indulging in so many grotesque gambols, that, in spite of the grave cause we had for seriousness, we could not help bursting into a hearty laugh.

Fritz leapt upon the onager and was preparing to set out in pursuit, when I stopped him, pointing out the danger he would incur in approaching the marsh, towards which the ass was now making as fast as he could.

We attempted to call the fugitive back, but he only looked round at us from time to time, shaking his mane with an air of bravado. We showed him fodder and salt: all was useless. He was evidently determined to enjoy his liberty, and, galloping further and further away, made straight for the supposed lair of the serpent.

All at once we saw a terrible head raise itself from among the reeds.

At sight of it the poor donkey appeared petrified with fear, uttered a strange, hopeless kind of groan, and looked towards us mournfully. One would have thought him transfixed to the earth, for as the serpent approached him he neither moved nor gave any indication that he even contemplated flight.

In an instant the unhappy beast was wrapped in the monster's fatal folds, and suffocated in the horrible embrace.

The children asked me if they might not fire upon the reptile, to release their favourite.

I forbade them, observing that they would only irritate the monster, which might perhaps turn its fury upon us without profit to the ass, who already gave no sign of life.

"Let us wait," I said, "till the boa has swallowed his victim, for when he is glutted with food there will no longer be any danger in attacking him, and we shall be sure of our prey."

"But," said Jack, "the frightful beast will not swallow our donkey at a mouthful, will he?"

"As serpents have no teeth to enable them to rend their prey," I replied, "they crush and swallow it at one and the same time. But look! see how the hideous creature is crushing the unfortunate animal's body with its rings, in order to bring it down to the size of its throat!"

As I spoke the boa was making ready his repast with horrible avidity.

Not only was the ass dead, but its body was crushed into a shapeless mass, of which one could distinguish nothing but the head hanging bleeding and hideous.

The boa, to get more strength, had twined his tail round a small jutting piece of rock, and was gradually pressing the broken flesh into a soft paste.

He then covered the whole carcase over with a slimy saliva, and, opening his enormous jaws, made ready to commence his repast.

He first laid himself out at full length in front of the mass he had so carefully kneaded. Then seizing the ass by the hind-legs, he began swallowing it, and, little by little, the thighs, the body, and the fore-legs were engulfed in the monster's body, which gave as many signs of pain as of pleasure as it swallowed the still bleeding mass.

When he came to the head, which he had neglected to crush, his hunger was appeased, and he rolled over completely motionless.

This was the moment I was waiting for.

Seizing my gun, I cried to my boys, "Courage, children! courage! The monster has fallen into our hands!"

I hastened towards the serpent, followed by Fritz and Jack, but not by Ernest, who, always more timid than his brothers, remained at the post of observation.

The boa keenly watched our approach, his eyes glistening with impotent malignity.

He was literally unable to move a muscle of his body. Fritz and I, therefore, had no difficulty in sending the contents of a couple of barrels, well loaded with bullets, crashing into his skull. An intensely evil light played in his eyes for a moment—his tail beat the ground feebly once or twice as he writhed in anguish—he was dead!

At this moment Jack, who desired to have his part in the victory, fired his pistol into the reptile's belly. The wound produced a kind of galvanic effect on the tail of the serpent, which flew up suddenly and struck our young giddy-head so smart a blow upon the chest that it knocked him down.

It is hardly necessary to say that, finding himself thus laid upon his back, he fully believed for the moment that the boa had come to life again, and trembled in every limb at the thought of following the donkey to his last resting place.

Happily this was the last evil deed for which our formidable enemy was responsible.

We sent up a shout of victory, which speedily brought my wife, with Ernest and Francis, upon the scene of action.

We embraced each other warmly in an ecstasy of joy. It seemed as if we had received a new lease of life.

"So far as I am concerned," said Ernest, always ready to display his erudition, "I honour our poor donkey for having devoted his life to our salvation, as those noble Roman heroes, the Curtii, did theirs for the citizens."

"What are we going to do with the body of the serpent?" asked Jack, recovering from his panic.

"Skin it and stuff it," said Ernest, "and put it in the museum as a trophy of our victory and a valuable curiosity."

"But," said Francis, "could not we eat this huge eel? We should have stews and broiled meats which would last us for weeks."

"Eat the flesh of a serpent!" exclaimed his mother—"of a serpent which is perhaps venomous!"

"The boa, my dear wife," I said, "is not venomous; and even if it were, there would be no danger in eating its flesh, provided we threw away the head. It is in that part of a serpent that the fangs and the glands are found which contain the poison."

CHAPTER 18

Excursion to the Farmery—The Cabiai—The Cinnamon-Apple

Satisfied that there were no snakes on the Goose Marsh side of the country, I determined that we should make an expedition to the farmery.

I had for a long time entertained the idea of fortifying this part of our domains.

We set out full of confidence and good spirits.

As it was our habit when we started on an expedition to give the goats, the sheep, and the poultry their liberty, my wife laid out plenty of food for them in the neighbourhood of Rock-house, to keep them together till we returned.

At last we were fairly on the road to Forest Grange, where we intended to pass the night. We determined to fill our bags with corn by the way, and to make a more detailed survey of Swan Lake and the neighbouring rice plantation.

There were no signs of our old enemies the monkeys.

Our farmery was in excellent condition. We dined with a good appetite, and after a substantial repast, set out to reconnoitre in the neighbourhood.

I took little Francis with me this time, arming him with a gun proportionate to his size, and teaching him how to carry, load, and fire it.

Ernest was left with his mother at the upper end of Swan Lake, which we were about to explore. Francis and I took the left bank, and Fritz and Jack the right.

As we could not think of setting out without the more nimble of our four-footed allies, each party was accompanied by a small detachment of them. Ernest and his mother had Fan and Nip; Turk and the jackal were with Fritz and Jack; Francis and I had Brown and Fawn for our companions.

Francis and I followed the left bank of the lake. We were much impeded in our progress by the underwood and reed-beds, but our dogs, on the contrary, ploughed through these obstacles with as much enjoyment as if they were in their native element.

All at once we heard a strange lowing sound in the reeds. It was so much like the muffled braying of an ass that Francis took it to be the young onager escaped from Rock-house.

"That cannot be," I said. "In the first place the animal is too young to bray so loudly. Secondly, it is impossible that he should have passed us without our seeing him. I am rather disposed to think it is a bittern, or a kind of heron called the marsh ox, because of its cry, which resembles the lowing of cattle in the distance."

Heron or bittern, Francis was impatient to fire his first shot at the extraordinary bird. In order to assist him in his very natural desire, I called the two dogs, and indicated to them the direction in which the heron lay.

In a few moments there was a rustling among the reeds, and almost immediately thereafter a report of a gun, followed by a cry of triumph on the part of my little sportsman. I doubted not that he had made a successful début.

I ran up to where the little fellow was standing proudly over his prize, which had just been retrieved by one of our young dogs. It was a cabiai, cavia, or cavy, about two feet six inches in length. This animal has short, stiff hair, very sleek, and of a blackish-brown colour, which becomes lighter as it reaches the belly. It lives upon aquatic plants, and can remain a long time under water.

When we were preparing to set out again, Francis, like a true sportsman, insisted upon carrying the cabiai slung over his shoulder. Unhappily, however, he was not strong enough to carry so heavy a burden.

"Ah! ah! I have it!" he cried at last. "I shall throw my game across the back of Brown, who seems, so far as I can judge, quite strong enough to carry it."

Francis, disembarrassed of his burden, which the honest Brown received upon his back with the utmost docility, set out again with the same vivacity and the same satisfaction that he had shown all along.

We soon reached Pine Wood, where we made a short halt, and then returned to Forest Grange without having lighted on any traces of the boa.

In returning to our good housewife we met Fritz and Jack, who did not appear to us to be very well satisfied with the results of their expedition. Nevertheless, Fritz brought in a pair of heathbirds, and Jack a dozen eggs wrapped up in a kind of fur.

The children, united again, talked over the results of their sport, speaking with enthusiasm of those of their exploits which had been successful, and passing lightly over their failures.

As to Francis's cabiai, it was cut up there and then. Part of it was placed upon the spit and eaten at once. The remainder was put by for the next day. We did not enjoy the flesh much: there was a marshy smell and taste about it.

Towards the end of the dinner, Ernest, always a young Sybarite, complained that we had nothing to take the abominable taste of the cabiai out of our mouths.

Fritz and Jack at once pounced upon their game-bags, and presented him with some pine-cone kernels, two little cocoa-nuts, and some light green apples which had a very agreeable smell.

"Stay! stay, boys, stay!" I cried. "What is this new fruit that Jack has brought us? Has he tasted it himself before offering it to his brother?"

"No, dear father," returned the young giddy-head. "I should have done so if Fritz had not stopped me, saying that it might possibly be the poisonous fruit of the mancinul. But it looks so delicious a fruit that I hope he is wrong."

While praising Fritz for his prudence and blaming Jack for his thoughtlessness, I cut open one of the unknown apples, remarking that, at all events, it did not resemble the mancinul inside, inasmuch as it contained no stone. Master Nip, approaching cunningly at this moment, snatched the half of the fruit which I had just cut off, and ate it up, at a convenient distance, with evident satisfaction.

This was taken as a general signal. All the boys pounced upon the fruit with so much avidity, that I had some difficulty in saving even one for my wife.

Ashamed of their greediness, the boys at once hastened to offer their mother what was left in their hands, which, truth to tell, was not much.

"Many thanks," said she, "for your kindness, but I have a whole apple here."

They blushed under the good-natured rebuke.

I questioned Jack anew as to the kind of tree from which he had gathered this delicious fruit. As I had supposed, it was the cinnamon of the Antilles.

I saw that sleep, the result of the fatigues of the day, was invading all four of the boys. I invited them to take their rest upon the cotton bags, and set them an example myself.

CHAPTER 19

*Halt at Sugar-Cane Grove—The Peccaries—An Otahitian
Roast—The Giant Bamboos—Continuation of Our Journey*

We awoke at daybreak, after a peaceful and refreshing sleep, and
renewed our journey in the direction of the plantation of sugar-
canes, to which we had given the name of Sugar-cane Grove. We had
previously constructed a hut there with the interlaced branches of
trees, and this did away with the necessity of putting up the tent
during the short time we expected to halt on our way.

Whilst my wife busied herself with preparing our breakfast, I and
my children scoured the neighbourhood, to see if there were
any traces of the boa. We returned without having discovered
any indication whatever of its passage through this part of our
domains.

We were hardly seated at table, regaling ourselves with fresh
sugar-canes, of which we had been deprived for some time, when we
were interrupted by the persistent barking of our dogs. We took our
guns, and ran towards a thicket of reeds, whence proceeded all the
tumult. After some minutes there appeared a number of little pigs,
which were running with all their strength, in a row one after the
other, like soldiers disciplined though routed. We had a fine time to
fire before they were out of reach. Three or four discharges from
our guns killed about a dozen of them, but did not interfere at all
with the methodical and rapid retreat of the troop. This uniformity
of movement, and the grey colour of the animals, convinced me that
we had before us a kind of wild pig, very different from the
European species. It was possible that they were musk-pigs or
peccaries.

As we were some distance from the hut where we had left my
wife, and as it was impossible to carry our spoils without the help
of our cart, I sent Jack to fetch it, and he was not long in bringing it
to us.

Whilst we were waiting I was not idle. Remembering to have

read somewhere that the flesh of the peccary is not good unless care is taken, as soon as it is dead, to remove its little scent-bag, I hastened to perform this necessary operation. When all was finished we packed our booty upon the cart, which we covered with flowers and green boughs, and returned to the hut singing joyously.

Notwithstanding the keenness of our appetites, the produce of this last hunt was too plentiful for us to finish it whilst the flesh was still sweet. It was therefore necessary to take some measures for its preservation.

While a special smoking-room was being constructed by Jack and Fritz, whom I entrusted with this duty, desiring them to make all speed, I cut off the hams and other choice parts of the animal, for future use. The carcases, as well as the heads, were left to the dogs and the eagle. The good flesh was carefully washed, salted, and placed in sacks open at the top, which we hung to the branches of the trees. A large gourd-vessel caught the drippings of salt water, which were poured over it again through the openings at the top.

The morning of the next day was employed in preparing an Otahitian roast, with which Fritz wished to surprise his mother. Under his direction his brothers dug out a cylindrical hole of a certain depth, in which they made a fire of branches and brushwood, so as to heat some stones. Whilst superintending the heating of his improvised oven, Fritz busied himself in the preparation of one of the pigs. He singed it, washed it, stuffed it with potatoes and sweet herbs, and finally salted it, not in the Otahitian, but in the European manner. I had told Fritz that, in default of banana-leaves, which are the best for this purpose, he had better envelop his animal in bark, so that it might be a little better protected against the dust and ashes; and, well for him, Fritz had scrupulously followed my recommendation.

The flesh, after having been prepared as I have described, was buried in a bed of red-hot stones, mixed with charcoal, wood-ashes, and earth; and whilst it was roasting quietly in this primitive oven, we returned to hasten the construction of the smoking-room, which we did not finish until evening. As soon as the hams were hung on the roof of the hut, which had been built by Fritz, we lighted upon a rude hearth, erected on the floor, a fire made up of damp turf and dry leaves, and it was not long before a thick smoke filled the hut, which we closed carefully in every part. I need not add that the smoke was kept up for several days, until the hams of the peccary were thoroughly penetrated by it.

Three hours sufficed to cook the Otahitian roast perfectly. When lifted out of the bed of earth, sand, and stones which covered it, there rose from the bottom of the hole in which it lay an agreeable savoury odour, which prepossessed us favourably, and which reconciled our good housewife to that which she had ironically called, some hours before, a barbarian piece of cookery. Fritz was triumphant. After the repast, as there was no reason why the stomach should not be grateful, I thought over the exquisite flavour which had been communicated to the dish by the bark I had advised my eldest son to use instead of the banana-leaves. I examined the bark and the tree which had produced it attentively, and came to the conclusion that it could be no other than the ravensara of Madagascar. In Madagascan language this word signifies "good leaf", and from this the botanists have given it the Greek name of Agathophyllum, which has the same signification. It unites to the perfume of the nutmeg that of cloves and cinnamon, and an oil is extracted from it with which Indian cooks flavour all their dishes.

The preparation of our hams kept us for two days near our smoking-room, and my wife, under the protection of one of our sons, kept the fire moderately replenished, whilst the rest of us made some excursions into the neighbourhood. Every time we returned, which was at mealtimes, we brought with us some booty. Amongst other treasures we discovered in the bamboo thicket a number of reeds about sixty feet in height, and proportionately thick, which we could easily use for casks, being careful to saw them near the knots. The thorns with which these knots were covered were as hard as nails, and were hailed by us with as much satisfaction as the reeds themselves. Also the young bamboo shoots, which we had gathered with the gigantic reeds, were specially appreciated by our good housewife, who preserved them in vinegar, covering them over with ravensara leaves.

On a journey to Prospect Hill, I saw with great disappointment that the monkeys had, as before, committed serious depredations at Forest Grange. The goats and sheep, too, had dispersed themselves in the neighbourhood, our fowls were become almost wild, and the cabin was in such a deplorable condition that I felt obliged to postpone to a future period the labour of repairing it.

Some days were employed in laying out our route, as well as in preserving the peccary flesh. When it seemed to us sufficiently smoked, we made ready to set out and continue our journey. We took some hams to increase our stock of provisions; the rest we put into the smoke-house, which we carefully barricaded with sand, earth, and thorns, to protect it from the attacks of birds of prey, wild beasts, and apes. Then, early one morning, our little caravan gaily set out.

CHAPTER 20

Excursions in the Savannah—The Herd of Ostriches and their
Eggs—The Green Valley—Fright of Ernest—The Bears

After a walk of some hours we arrived, without adventure, upon the outskirts of a small wood. The situation was charming, and well sheltered. The wood was bounded on the right by a steep rock, and on the left by the mouth of a river which emptied itself into the large bay. Within the distance of a gunshot lay the narrow defile, between the river and the rocks, which gave access to our domains. It was an agreeable and advantageous position from every point of view. We pitched our tent, and made the necessary arrangement for a more lengthened stay there. During the preparations for dinner I proposed an excursion into the wood, to assure ourselves that we had no unpleasant neighbours, and we met with nothing worse than some wild cats, which were occupied in hunting badgers, and which fled at our approach.

After dinner the heat became so suffocating that we could not dream of undertaking anything. The evening was spent in preparations and projects for the following days, principally for the morrow, when we intended taking a longer excursion than any we had hitherto made. At sunrise we were ready, my three eldest sons and I, and having taken breakfast we set off, escorted by our fourlegged skirmishers, Fan excepted. In passing through the defile we saw our barricade of bamboos broken and overturned, doubtless by the late hurricanes and inundations, and we concluded that it must have been by this opening that the boa had entered our domains. We forded the stream, whose shores appeared to us still pleasanter when, seated on the eastern bank, we saw the side of the mountains covered with clusters of shrubs smiling with verdure. But as we advanced the country grew more barren and arid. There was not a single trace of water. The grass became scarcer and scarcer. The only plants which we saw were dry, thorny, and without beauty; indeed, such as one would expect to find upon a soil so scorched. Fortunately, we had taken the precaution to fill our gourds at the stream before leaving it behind us.

After a painful walk of two hours, during which my three young companions had only opened their parched mouths to rail against the heat and the fatigue, we arrived at the foot of a hill which we had fixed upon as the furthest point of our journey. Here, with no desire to go further, we sat down under the shade of a rock for rest and refreshment.

All at once Fritz, who, whilst eating, was looking attentively before him, rose suddenly.

"What do I see below?" cried he. "It looks like two men on horseback. A third is approaching them at a gallop. They are coming in our direction. Father, can it be the Arabs of the desert?"

"It is impossible, my dear boy," replied I. "However, as we cannot be too prudent, take my telescope and look attentively. What do you see now?"

"I see a large herd of cattle grazing here and there; then some haycocks walking, and loaded waggons which go and come from the wood to the river. What can all this be, father?"

I smilingly took the telescope, and told my three boys, who were much excited by the adventure, that what they took for mounted cavaliers on large horses were only giant ostriches, to which, if they liked, we would give chase, since we had so fine an opportunity. They agreed with pleasure.

The ostriches came nearer and nearer to us. I resolved to wait and surprise them, if that were possible. I therefore ordered Fritz to call in the dogs and the ape, whilst Ernest and I hid ourselves in a crevice of the rock, where Fritz and Jack, leading our animals, soon joined us.

We could see the ostriches very distinctly, and they gradually drew near to us. There were five, four of which were females, the male being easily distinguished by his white feathers.

"My dear boys," said I, "if we intend to capture one of these creatures we must be careful not to startle them, for we could not dream of hunting an animal which could beat a horse at full gallop. Our eagle alone can match them in flight."

The ostriches had now approached to within a hundred paces of us. On seeing us they stopped, looking disquieted and irresolute; but as we kept in the dogs, and ourselves remained all but immovable, they took courage and innocently came to meet us, swaying their necks first on this side and then on that, examining us with an air of mingled curiosity and astonishment which was very amusing. They might have familiarised themselves with our appearance, and came close enough for us to capture them by means of the lasso, if our dogs, who were very impatient, had not at this moment escaped and thrown themselves upon the ostriches with a great noise of yelping and barking. Like feathers carried away by the wind, the ostriches dispersed over the plain, using their wings as sails. They had the appearance of ships sailing over an immense sea of sand. In a few minutes they had vanished out of sight.

Fritz meanwhile, following my recommendation, had quickly unbound the eyes of his eagle, and let him loose at the moment the ostriches took flight.

The male, which we admired more than all on account of his beauty, was a little in the rear of the rest—for the purpose, no doubt, of protecting his companions. This circumstance proved fatal to him. Fritz's eagle precipitated himself upon him, struck him in the neck, and knocked him down in less time than I can tell. The jackal continued the work. We came up just in time to secure a few feathers for our hats.

We then continued our journey. Before long, Ernest and Jack, who were walking in front, stopped and called to us with all their might.

"Come quickly!" cried they. "An ostrich's nest! an ostrich's nest!"

We ran, and there we saw in a hole in the sand about twenty eggs, as white as ivory and as large as the head of a child.

"It is a splendid find," said I; "but do not disturb the order in which these eggs are placed; for fear the hen should abandon them when she returns."

"Do you not think they are abandoned?" said Fritz.

"No," said I. "In this scorching climate the ostrich generally leaves her eggs to the heat of the sun in the daytime, and returns to cover them during the night."

The children could not, however, resist the temptation of taking one or two of these eggs to show to their mother. I therefore lifted two, which were on the top of the others, as gently as possible, and after having raised a little pile of stones, to enable us to find the nest again, we went on our way.

By degrees we approached the cavern where Jack had caught his young jackal.

We were only a short distance from it, when we saw the valiant Ernest come running towards us, pale and agitated, accompanied by his friend Fawn. He had set out on his own account to take possession of the cavern, in which we had determined to rest awhile.

"A bear, father! a bear!" cried he in a voice tremulous with fear, and he threw himself into my arms, clasping me closely, as if begging my protection. Ernest's fright had a serious cause, for with the barks of our dogs were mixed growls of a by no means doubtful nature. I pressed forward, gun in hand, recommending courage and prudence to my children.

In a few moments a huge bear dashed out of the cavern, with a dog hanging to each ear; behind him came another, still larger.

Fritz, who followed me closely, chose this last for his adversary, whilst I prepared to do battle with the first. Jack, a little agitated but ready to do his part, stood a short distance off. Ernest alone, I am sorry to say, failed to form one of our group. He had not yet recovered from his emotion.

Fritz and I fired together. Unfortunately, neither of our shots was mortal, for, being afraid of wounding one of our dogs, who pulled their dangerous enemies hither and thither, and at times seemed to form part of them, we could not choose a spot to aim at. Still, I had shattered the jaw of one of the bears, and Fritz had broken one of the fore-feet of the other, so that if they were not precisely unable to fight at all, they were both rendered rather less formidable. However, the two bears continued to defend themselves energetically—sometimes seated, sometimes upright—menacing us, and filled with rage, which expressed itself in growls that resounded in echoes through the cavern.

It was necessary to finish the combat, for if prolonged it might have proved fatal to our courageous companions. I loaded one of my pistols, and, advancing a few steps, I chose the moment when the head of one of the bears was exposed, and quick as lightning fired a ball at it; while Fritz, not less fortunate than myself, hit the other one in the heart.

"God be praised!" cried I earnestly, seeing our two enemies fall down in the last agonies of death.

Jack, who had witnessed our victory, ran joyously to announce it to Ernest, and persuaded him to approach the scene of conflict.

"Why," said I, without thinking of reproaching his inaction in the face of danger, "were you so eager to go first into the cavern?"

"Father," he replied in a guilty tone of voice, "God has punished me, for I only went in there with the intention of concealing myself, to frighten Jack by imitating the growlings of a bear. I never thought that two real bears would come to enact naturally a part which I was only intending to play as a joke."

These animals were in truth terrible. One, the largest, measured about eight feet in length, and the other rather more than six. Their powerful paws, their strong shoulders, their enormous necks, their glistening hides, which shone with a metallic lustre, excited the admiration of my boys, who, seated on the two still warm carcases, occupied themselves by examining them in detail. We certainly had before us two examples of the silver bear met with by Captain Clarke, on the north-west coast of America. However that might be, the skins of these beasts would furnish us with magnificent furs. But, as it was impossible for us to skin them at once, I contented myself with dragging the two bodies into the cavern, whose entrance we closed up with a thick trellis-work of branches.

Fritz and Jack left the ostrich's eggs there also, as the weight inconvenienced them; for it was late, and we should have to make all haste to return to our hut before nightfall.

CHAPTER 21

The Condor—Skinning and Curing the Bears—An Expedition by the
Four Boys—The Angora Rabbits—The Antelopes—Fritz's
Narrative—The Cuckoo—Jack and the Bees

A little before daybreak on the following morning, I got up—not
without a sharp struggle with a certain degree of lassitude, very
excusable after the labours of the preceding day—and called the
family.

Breakfast finished and the oxen harnessed, we set out for Bear
Cavern, which we reached without accident.

Fritz—who, as usual, led the van of our little caravan—cried out,
the moment he got in sight of the entrance to the cavern, "Make
haste! pray make haste, if you wish to see a regiment of turkeys! I do
not know whether they have assembled to do honour to the funeral
of our huge enemies; but there is a fine proud fellow up in front
there, who seems to be a sort of royal guard, keeping away the crowd
of humbler people from the place where the two sovereigns of the
forest are lying in state."

That which Fritz had termed the royal guard was a bird of high
stature, with a bright red comb, long wattles clinging like a strip of
flesh to its neck, a collar of white feathers falling upon its breast, and
a bare pink neck, much wrinkled. His plumage was black, flecked
here and there with white.

He paced gravely up and down in front of the cavern, which he
entered from time to time, as if to superintend the arrangements for
some ceremony there.

We were contemplating this strange spectacle with the utmost
astonishment, when we heard a great noise in the air over our heads.
We looked up, and saw a huge bird with an immense spread of
wings.

In an instant it fell among the turkeys, pierced by a ball which Fritz
had sent after it.

The feathered band, which we had seen assembled together at the entrance to the grotto, at once took wing and dispersed in all directions. The large bird, the supposed guardian of the dead, alone remained, contemplating with his great round eyes the body of his newly-arrived friend, upon which our dogs were on the point of precipitating themselves.

He was not slow, however, to follow the example just set him by his companions. He started off at full speed, and there was left us only the bird Fritz had shot and a turkey which it had crushed in its fall.

I entered the cavern cautiously, and soon found that the tongue and eyes of one of our bears had disappeared. A few hours later, and their magnificent furs and succulent hams would have been lost to us to the manifest advantage of the aerial marauders which we had just dispersed.

I returned to the two dead birds, and, after an attentive examination, I came to the conclusion that that which we had taken for a turkey was a vulture found in Brazil, where it is called the uruhu, and that which Fritz had killed was a condor, as indeed was shown by the extraordinary size of its wings.

We spent the remainder of the day in skinning the bears, a labour which we found to be very unpleasant and very difficult. To complete it took us two days, during which time we bivouacked in the tent that we had erected a few steps from the mouth of the cavern.

Yielding to their earnest solicitations, I permitted Fritz, Jack, and even little Francis, who loved adventure as ardently as his brothers, to undertake with their dogs an expedition to the savannah, while I, contrary to my habit, remained at the tent with my wife and Ernest.

While my active wife, assisted by Ernest, proceeded with the curing of the bears' flesh, I found plenty of occupation in the cavern.

I had remarked, during a careful examination, that the interior rock was formed of a species of mica, traversed by long threads of amianth. I proceeded to dig, and was not long in finding sheets of the former mineral, as much as two feet square, and transparent as crystal. It was a most valuable discovery, for henceforth we had a kind of glass with which to glaze our windows in lieu of the fish-glue, or isinglass, which was useless in the wind and rain.

Towards the evening while we were grilling a few appetising slices of bears' flesh, and growing somewhat uneasy at the prolonged absence of our young huntsmen, a sound of distant hoofs and a faint echo of hurrahs borne upon the wind announced the return of the excursionists.

I went to meet them. They leapt from their beasts at once, unsaddled them, set them free to depasture themselves, and walked home with me to the tent.

Jack and Francis each carried a kid slung over his shoulder.

Fritz's game-bag was of a size that looked significant.

"Splendid sport, father! splendid sport!" cried the lively Jack. "Do you see these kids?"

"Yes, to say nothing of the Angora rabbits which Fritz has in his game-bag!" added Francis precipitately.

"Yes, and to say nothing either of——" Jack was saying, with even more precipitation, when——

"Stay!" I cried. "Stay! proceed in order, pray. Let Fritz begin: he will be able, I doubt not, to give us a correct account of your adventures."

Fritz went on to tell his story.

"An hour after we left you," he said, "we crossed Green Valley at a brisk trot, passed through a ravine to the great plain, and found ourselves upon an eminence which commanded the surrounding country. From the spot on which we stood we could see the rocky defile, where a number of animals, which I believed to be either gazelles, goats, or antelopes, were quietly feeding. We determined to give chase to them. I led the way cautiously, and in order to avoid frightening the game we held our dogs in leash.

"Arrived within a short distance, Francis took a course to the left, Jack rode straight on, while I, mounted on the onager, set off to the right to cut off the retreat of any animal which should try to escape us. We advanced cautiously and quickly, you may be sure; but, in spite of that, the herd took alarm. Several of them bounded from rock to rock, staying every now and then to toss their heads and prick up their ears. At this point we let the dogs loose, and galloped after them at full speed.

"Distracted by the unusual sight and sounds, the poor creatures sought safety in flight; but we had so ordered our plans that, start from where they would, they were compelled eventually to pass through the place we had chosen for them—that is to say, the defile. The first difficulty was over, but it now became necessary to devise some plan of turning our conquest to account. We determined to make the herd prisoners in the defile, and drive them home to

Farm Grange. And this is how we did it: We stretched a piece of string across the road about three or four feet from the ground, and tied upon it the ostrich feathers which we had in our caps, and some pieces of rag that were lying in the bottom of our game-bags. The wind blew these about, and the animals as soon as they saw them came to a dead stand, not knowing which way to turn. I had read of something similar being done in an account of a voyage made by Captain Levaillant, the naturalist, and I thought I might as well try my hand at the experiment. It was perfectly successful."

"Well done, brave boy!" I said, interrupting him. "I am happy to see that you have profited by your reading. Now tell me how you took the Angora rabbits, and tell me also what you propose to do with them. I warn you that I am not very much disposed to admit them to our domains, for they multiply almost to infinity, and will prove very injurious to our fields and gardens."

"The capture of these rabbits," said Fritz, "is due to my eagle, which pounced down upon a flock of them that were frisking at the foot of a little hill. He brought me two alive and one dead which latter I gave him to eat for his trouble. As to the introduction of them into what you call our domains, have we not two little islands at our disposal which we could people with these pretty little animals without any danger or loss to ourselves whatever? We should thus be assured of a delicacy for our table, and fur for our caps and other garments."

"You speak wisely, my son," I replied, "and as you seem to be both able and willing to carry out your plan, I will leave its execution wholly in your hands."

"Is it not our turn to speak now?" asked Jack, who was growing very impatient.

"Undoubtedly," I replied, smiling. "Let us hear how you brought down these beautiful kids."

"By hunting—sheer hunting!" he cried excitedly. "Fritz was some distance off, engaged with his eagle and the rabbits. Our dogs were sniffing about in the underwood, when they put up two animals resembling large hares. They took to flight instantly, bounding and capering in the most extraordinary manner. We and our dogs followed them at the top of our speed. In about a quarter of an hour they were out of breath, and fell down as if they were dead. We got down from our cattle, drove away the dogs, and found that what we had supposed to be large hares were young kids. We tied them by the legs and slung them over our shoulders. There! that is the history of the day's sport so far as Francis and I are concerned."

"Good, my children!" I said, "you have done well. The only remark I would make is that the kids, as you term them, are very fine specimens of the dwarf antelope. And now, Jack, I want you to explain how it is that your face is so swollen? Have you been fighting a legion of mosquitoes?"

"Oh, no," said Jack gaily, "my wounds are more honourable than that. I will tell you how I came by them. We were all three returning home, when I noticed a bird that kept flying from tree to tree in front of us, and seemed to invite us by his song to follow him. I thought the bird was playing us some impudent trick, and put my gun to my shoulder to take aim at it, when Fritz stopped me, observing that it was of no use to fire, as my gun was loaded with a bullet: small shot, he said, was the only thing for such a bird as that at such a distance. 'Besides,' he added, 'the bird resembles the Indicator cuckoo spoken of by Buffon and Latham, and it may be giving us counsel that it would be well to take.'

"Upon that we determined to follow the bird, at all events for a short distance. After a few minutes it settled on a tree and ceased its song. We stopped also, and were not long in discovering that the trunk of the tree upon which it had posted itself was the retreat of a swarm of bees. The bird, which lives upon honey, no doubt coveted that store which it knew was concealed within, and, as its habit is, led us to the place where it was in the hope that we should leave it part of our booty in repayment for its services.

"We were trying to hit upon some means of taking the bees, when Fritz proposed to suffocate them with a sulphur match, as you had done. I lighted one at once, and without stopping to plug up the hole threw it in among the buzzing colony. In a moment the whole swarm poured out and set upon me. I was assailed in so many places at once and saw such clouds of fresh enemies pouring down upon me, that it seemed as if all the bees in the world were at my heels. They stung and tormented me until there was nothing left but to leap upon my buffalo and make off at the top of my speed. That is the story. You see the state I am in. It is not my fault, for I rubbed myself with damp earth as soon as I could get clear of my enemies, remembering that was the remedy which you applied when I was attacked by bees before."

My wife dressed the poor boy's face and neck with salt-water bandages, which relieved his pain and left him free to make a hearty supper.

Afterwards, assisted by the other boys, I made a sort of cage in which to transport the Angora rabbits, first to Rock-house and then to Shark Island.

Then we retired to rest.

CHAPTER 22

Spurge-oil—Arab Hill—Capture of an Ostrich—The Return to
Rock-house—Another Large Eel—Training the
Ostrich—Hydromel—Hat-Making

There were many things still remaining to be done before our return
to Rock-house—a return which it was necessary to hasten for more
than one reason, the most important being the approaching recur-
rence of the rainy season.

Our bears' flesh had been salted and smoked; but I did not wish to
leave behind either the ostrich-eggs which we had found, or some
spurge-oil which I had lighted upon in a little wood during one of
our expeditions.

I determined, therefore, to make a final excursion into the
savannah.

We set out, leaving at home with our good housewife, not little
Francis, who desired to distinguish himself in our company, but the
indolent Ernest, who now made no secret of his distaste for fatiguing
journeys.

Fritz on this occasion handed over to me his onager, and
himself mounted young Swift, her foal, which was destined to
become an excellent hack. Francis mounted his calf, and Jack his
buffalo.

Brown and Fawn very much wished to accompany us, but I
thought it better to leave them behind for the protection of my wife,
and I told Ernest to look after them.

We took the Green Valley road, but in an opposite direction to
Bear Cave, and eventually came to Arab Hill—the name we gave to
the eminence from the top of which we had at first mistaken the
ostriches for mounted Arabs.

Arrived there, I permitted Jack and Francis to push on ahead, but
without losing sight of them for an instant.

As to Fritz, he stopped with me to assist in securing a supply of
spurge-oil from the trunks of the euphorbia shrub, in which I had
been careful to make incisions when I was there before. The sun had

dried the exudations, of which we collected a large quantity, and placed it in some bamboo vessels that we had brought for the purpose.

This valuable harvest achieved, we set out to overtake our advance guard, who had got far beyond the ostrich-nest without knowing it. The two boys were strongly desirous of knocking over some of these couriers of the savannah, as well as of taking one or two alive for their brother Fritz, who had often expressed a wish to possess one. He now determined to join in the chase, and obtained my leave to remount the onager for the purpose.

We had not long to wait for the result of the sport. Before we had advanced far, four ostriches—three females and a male—came out of the thicket in which our nest lay.

As they made straight towards us, they fell in with our young companions, who were accompanied by their dogs. There was but little chance of their escaping us.

When they were fairly within range, I threw my lasso at one of them; but the cord, instead of getting entangled in the legs of the creature, at which point I aimed it, entwined itself round the upper part of the body. The motion of the wings was at once paralysed, but the vigorous animal began struggling fiercely to disembarrass itself of the ill-adjusted cord; and I feel certain it would have escaped me if Fritz had not immediately dispatched his eagle, whose beak he had bound with cotton in order that it might not seriously wound our victim.

The eagle pounced upon the ostrich, laid hold of it by the top of the head, and arrested it in its impetuous course.

Jack, arriving at a gallop, threw his lasso, and, more adroit than I was, succeeded in entangling the legs of the animal, which fell heavily upon its side.

To rush up and bind it more securely was the work of an instant. After having tied a handkerchief over its head—a precaution without which we should never have been able to master it—I strapped its wings down with a strip of dog-fish skin, through which I passed a strong cord. One end of this cord I attached to the collar of Storm, the other to that of Grumbler. I had determined that the bird should be thus led home between the two oxen; and, as I did not wish that its kicking and struggling should in any way incommode these two faithful servants, I fettered its legs in such wise that it could walk with tolerable ease without having the power to do any harm. These precautions taken, I removed the handkerchief with which I had blindfolded it, and the lasso-ropes which pained it unnecessarily, and awaited the result.

At first, irritated and humiliated at finding itself vanquished, the bird remained absolutely immovable upon the ground. Then, fancying itself free again, it all at once leaped up and tried to take wing. But the straps and cords held it back, and it fell upon its knees.

It was soon up again, struggling furiously; but, thanks to the strong necks and shoulders of Storm and Grumbler, it strove in vain. At length, being powerless to do otherwise, it gave up the unequal contest, and submitted to follow the gentler forward movement of its two brave conductors.

While Jack and Francis, mounted upon their oxen, led our captive to Arab Hill, Fritz and I made our way to the ostrich-nest which we had discovered during a former visit to the spot. We were not many paces from it, when a female ostrich rose from the eggs so unexpectedly that we had time neither to fire at nor follow it before it was far beyond our reach.

The bird's presence there proved clearly that the nest had not been abandoned, and we had some hope that we might find among the eggs at least one or two that were far enough advanced to be hatched artificially. We carried away ten of them, leaving the others buried in the sand, in order that the mother upon her return might continue her maternal office.

We carefully slung our spoils to our saddles, and rejoined our young companions, with whom we set out for Bear Cavern, passing through Green Valley on the way.

On our return we were at first saluted with cries of admiration. But soon our good housewife grew alarmed at the bare thought of the prodigious quantity of food which our prisoner would devour.

"My good husband!" she exclaimed, "to what possible use can you put this huge glutton that will repay the drain it will cause upon our scanty stock of provisions during the rainy season?"

"It will supply me with a swift steed," said Jack, with enthusiasm; "and if our little country is joined anywhere to the continent of Asia or Africa, I will, thanks to our ostrich, make a journey thither in a few days, to seek help and news of our fatherland of the first European colony that I meet with. In anticipation of its future exploits, therefore, I name it 'Tornado'; for it shall travel as swiftly, or I have no skill in ostrich-breaking. So soon as he shall be taught to obey the bit, I will be his rider, and Ernest shall have my dear buffalo, Storm."

After a little pouting and recrimination on the part of Francis, the ostrich was unanimously awarded to Jack, who from that moment took possession of it and began its education.

It was too late today to think of returning to Forest Grange; but early the next morning we were all on the way thither, human beings and cattle.

The ostrich marched with bandaged eyes between the two oxen. The car was harnessed to the cow, on whose back Ernest rode. Jack and Francis naturally mounted Storm and Grumbler. I was upon Lightfoot, and Fritz upon Swift. My wife rode on the car. Altogether we formed a highly picturesque caravan.

Directly we reached the farmery we unharnessed our beasts, partook of a hasty supper of cold meat, and flung ourselves upon our beds of cotton; for we were worn-out utterly by fatigue.

At daybreak I went out to the poultry, and saw with pleasure that among the chickens hatched by our hens were several fine fat pullets. My wife desired to carry these to Rock-house, our favourite dwelling-place, towards which we seemed to be drawn after our long absence by a kind of nostalgia, or home-sickness.

While the two younger boys were helping their mother, I proceeded with two others to the unpacking and provisional stowing away of our booty.

The ostrich, relieved of the bonds which attached it to the oxen, was tied up in front of our dwelling, under the arbour of branches, where I decided it was to remain until properly tamed.

The ostrich-eggs were placed in tepid water for some time; and those in which we believed there were young were afterwards placed on a cushion of cotton, and deposited in the oven, which, with the aid of a thermometer, I raised to the necessary temperature for their incubation.

The Angora rabbits were the same day transported and left on Shark Island, where their mission was to acclimatise themselves and propagate their species. We resolved to pay them a visit soon, and prepare them a proper dwelling-place for the rainy season.

In our new division of territory, Whale Island fell to the dwarf antelopes, which, though nearly dead when taken, revived, and with care became as strong and active as ever. We were particularly desirous of keeping these graceful creatures in our immediate neighbourhood; but we feared that the dogs, unable to withstand so tempting a prey, might worry them when we were out of sight.

As to some land-turtles which we had found in the vicinity of Sugar-cane Grove, and of which we had left a couple at Forest Grange, I at first thought of turning them loose in the kitchen-garden to rid it of snails that infested it. But as my wife had less fear of the ravages of the latter than of the damage which the turtles might do among the young plants, I told Jack to go and place them among the reeds in Goose Marsh.

The boy carried the creatures off at once. Scarcely had he reached his destination, when I heard him calling for Fritz at the top of his voice, saying, "Make haste, Fritz! Pray make haste! And bring a stick with you!"

I thought at first that it was some frog-hunting freak, for there were a great many of these creatures in the marsh, and Jack liked nothing better than to pursue them till they leapt souse into the water. Great was my surprise, therefore, to see the boys returning with a magnificent eel, which had been taken upon a line secretly laid by Ernest before we set out on our excursion. A portion of the delicious fish was immediately prepared for our dinner. The remainder was preserved in butter and salt for a future occasion.

We undertook the training of Tornado (this, the reader will remember, was the name Jack gave to the ostrich); but I am bound to confess that we did not at first succeed very well therein.

I was obliged to stupefy the poor creature with the fumes of tobacco, as Ernest had done with Fritz's eagle. When she was in this state the children mounted her in turn, to accustom her to the weight of their bodies and the novelty of being ridden after the manner of a horse. This she permitted us to do, not having any will of her own during the existence of the state of torpor into which the tobacco threw her. But in spite of our patience and perseverance, in spite of our caresses, in spite of the excellent litter we had provided for her, in spite of the care we had taken day by day to lengthen the cord with which she was attached in order to give her more liberty as an earnest of still greater freedom in the future, she remained quite intractable. The poor creature, indeed, refusing all nourishment, seemed at last to have resolved to perish of hunger, to punish us for having separated her from her companions in the savannah.

She became so feeble and wretched that I began to fear we should not rear her, and to regret that we had ever deprived her of her native freedom. Happily my wife one morning hit upon a plan of relieving us of our difficulties. She prepared some balls of bruised maize and butter, such as they fatten capons with; and these we gave to the ostrich, who swallowed them eagerly. From this day the creature ate everything we placed before it. So robust did its appetite become, indeed, that our fears underwent an entire change. From doubting whether it would live, we came to doubt whether we should be able to find food enough for its support. Fortunately, however, about this time Madame Tornado took to alternating pebbles with her other food—a fact which led the boys to think that she might probably come to eating pebbles altogether, till I told them that she swallowed stones only for digestive purposes.

Her strength thus revived, her education was proceeded with vigorously. In less than a month, she knew how to sit down, get up, turn, walk, trot, and gallop at the command of her young driver, Jack.

As we desired to use her as a riding-horse, it was necessary to make her a bit and bridle; and I was much embarrassed to know what to do in the matter. A bit was indispensable to guide her with; but who ever saw a bit adapted to a beak?

I was on the point of giving the thing up, when I recollected to have noticed that the alternation of light and shade had a great influence over her; and I conceived the idea of making for her a leathern hood, something like one which Fritz had made after the manner of falconers to manoeuvre his eagle. Bringing the cap far enough down the neck to fasten it securely, I cut in it two square flaps like the blinkers of a horse's bridle, and these I attached to reins which could easily be managed by the rider. By shutting one of the blinkers, the ostrich would at once be turned in the direction of the other whence the light came. By shutting both, she would be stopped altogether. By opening both, she would be directed straight ahead.

The equipment of the ostrich finished, we tried her capabilities, which were beyond our expectations. If she declined to do much as a draught beast, she justified her name of Tornado by her performances as a saddle-horse. She accomplished, for instance, the journey between Falcon-nest and back again before Fritz upon his onager was able to traverse more than half the distance.

So superior, indeed, was she in speed to any of our other animals, that Fritz, Ernest and Francis grew jealous of Jack, her master, and begged me to withdraw the gift we had made him. But I held steadfastly to our first decision, and Jack continued to retain possession of his ostrich, which, however, was none the less the property of his three brothers, for they rode it almost as often as they pleased, and were allowed equal rights in its services when they required them.

The preparation of the bears' skins had proceeded simultaneously with the training of the ostrich and other small labours. In place of bark, I tanned them with a vinegar made of honey; and for a fleshing-knife, I used the blade of an old sabre. To soften them and render them fit for use as leather, I rubbed them well with a compound of grease and ashes, which produced the precise effect intended.

Speaking of this vinegar, I may mention here in passing that while making it for the use I have mentioned, I obtained, without any intention of doing so, an excellent hydromel, or honey-water. The attempt to achieve the useful had brought forth the agreeable, and henceforth my boys and I were assured of a refreshing drink during our thirst-producing daily labours.

My double success as tanner and distiller emboldened me. I took a turn at the trade of the hatter, and essayed to make a beaverhat of the skins of the musk-rats for little Francis. As, however, this was a kind of industry for which none of my previous occupations had fitted me, I at first failed to achieve my ends. But I was not thereby discouraged. After several attempts, I obtained a sort of felt, to which, for want of a more sober dye, I imparted a brilliant red colour obtained from the cochineal insect. To render the fabric impervious to wet, I impregnated it with caoutchouc. When it was thus prepared, I moulded it upon a block, and placed it in the oven for a night to dry. The next morning we had the satisfaction of drawing out a magnificent red Swiss biretta, light in weight, and sufficiently strong for all reasonable wear.

My wife, delighted to witness the pleasure with which Francis contemplated his new cap, added thereto a lining of silk, a band of gold lace, and a plume of ostrich-feathers.

At first the child was not at all at ease in his new hat: its brilliancy contrasted so ludicrously with the old caps worn by myself and his brothers. I was, therefore, obliged to promise that I would make similar birettas for the whole family provided the brothers would supply me with the skins.

They brought enough to make fifty hats.

CHAPTER 23

Return of the Rainy Season—Manufacture of Pottery—Building a Cajack—Voyage to Shark Island

My success as a hatter induced me to seek new laurels as a potter. I had first to make models in wood—a work which, owing to my unskilfulness as a turner, was at least but imperfectly done; and then upon these I had to mould others, which were eventually to become the utensils we desired to manufacture. Then I occupied myself in stuffing the condor and the vulture. I laid the skins to soak in tepid water, into which I threw a little of the gum of the spurge-tree, to prevent the future ravages of insects. Thus softened and rendered impervious to corruption, I stretched them over pieces of wood, carved out in the form of the birds to be represented. Small rods, covered with cotton wire, were placed in the neck, while the wings were supported in their proper positions with the aid of wire. For eyes I made four small balls of porcelain, of the requisite size, which I painted and baked, and which restored to the two birds their natural appearance.

For all this, however, we were not able to while away the monotony of the long days.

Fritz came to the rescue.

"Now," said he, "that we have in the ostrich a rapid traveller, by land, we ought, I think, to have another for a sphere a little more extended. I mean the sea. What if we were to make a Greenland canoe, or cajack?"

I fell in with the proposition at once; it was hailed by the youngsters with enthusiasm; but my dear wife received it with a sigh of apprehension. Completely ignorant of what a cajack was, she dreaded that we were about engaging in an imprudent enterprise. I tried to reassure her by explaining that a cajack was a wonderfully safe kind of canoe, covered with the skin of the dog-fish and very strong and buoyant. Hearing this, she was constrained to give her assent to our project, in spite of the aversion with which any vessel designed to traverse the sea inspired her.

We set to work at once, in order to have, at least, the body of the canoe finished before the return of the fine season. First of all, with the aid of our largest whale-bones, which were of a curved shape naturally, and which I joined together end to end, I made two keels fitting into each other and of about twelve feet in length.

I gave them a coat of resin, and underneath cut three holes, into which I fitted some small castors to facilitate the transport of the skiff on land. I then fastened the two keels securely together with bamboos, and ran up at each end a new whalebone, which was intended to form the prow and stern of the cajack. I also bound the keels together with a band of copper, to which I fixed an iron ring for mooring purposes. Split bamboos served to build up the sides of the vessel, excepting the higher parts of it, which I formed of reeds similar to those which grew in Goose Marsh. I also worked some of these reeds in amongst the split bamboos, and so shaped the vessel to my liking. The deck extended over the whole surface of the cajack. I cut a circular opening in it for the oarsman, and round the opening placed a rim over which he could fasten his waterproof cape, and so keep the sea from entering the hole. In an ordinary cajack, the Greenlander who rows it is obliged to kneel during the process—a fatiguing position if long continued. Among other innovations upon the ordinary form of the boat, I placed in the opening a movable seat, which the occupant could either use or not as he pleased.

The body of our canoe was finished. Owing, perhaps, to the seat, it was a little higher than it should have been; but happily that modification did not appear to affect its lightness or its elasticity.

Much as we had accomplished, our task was but half completed. After having carefully caulked all the joints with a mixture of tar and moss, we covered the skeleton of the boat inside and out with two of our largest dog-fish skins, so as to cover over the bamboos and reedwork.

Dog-fish skins were also strained over the deck, and fastened down by bamboos, which formed two bulwarks to the boat. I forgot to say that the hole cut in the deck for the rower was placed a little farther back than is usual, because I wished to put up a mast forward. For the present the skiff had to be rowed with a paddle, to one of whose blades I fastened a bladder coated with wax, the better to assist its occupant in swimming to shore should he be capsized.

At length, to the general satisfaction, the cajack was finished. But before I could permit its owner, who could be none other than he who had at first conceived the idea of making it, to venture to sea, I begged my wife to try all her ingenuity to the utmost to make him a suitable swimming dress. This dress, by my advice, was to be so constructed as to form a covering adapted to the size and shape of the hole in the deck, and to envelop the rower completely—of course, leaving his movements unfettered. Besides this, as it was necessary to provide against every contingency, the dress was made double throughout, so that air could be injected into it by means of a small tube provided with a stopper. The rower would thus be able to inflate himself like a balloon, and to float on the surface of the water by his own specific gravity.

At last, on a fine afternoon, our strange craft was launched into the sea. Fritz, in order to honour the life-coat which I had devised and my wife had made, put it on, inflated it, and walked boldly into the water, where he floated as securely as if he had been walking on land. His brothers were as much amused as astonished at the strange figure he made, and because of the protuberances which the coat made both before and behind, laughingly gave him the nickname of Punch.

Following Fritz in our pirogue, we made a tour round the island. We found an unusual quantity of sea-wrack and other marine plants, of which the boys carried away several armfuls.

On our return to Deliverance Bay, my wife selected from amongst the plants several serrated leaves of about six or seven inches long, which she carefully washed and spread in the sun to dry, afterwards placing them in our oven with a sort of mysterious solemnity; on which I bantered her, but without, for the moment, obtaining any satisfactory explanation. Some days afterwards, when we had returned wearied, hungry, and thirsty from a tour of Falcon-nest, the dear woman set before us, in a large gourd-dish, the finest transparent jelly we had ever seen. It was neither more nor less than the product of the famous leaves which my wife had prepared unknown to us in order to give us a surprise. I leave you to judge whether her ruse succeeded, and also to imagine the avidity with which we fell-to upon the new dish. My wife told us afterwards that she had recognised amongst the marine plants some leaves similar to those which she had seen prepared with sugar and the juice of citron, or of orange, by the housewives of the cape where we put in for a time during the ill-fated voyage which brought us to these parts. She had simply substituted for the citron, which alone was lacking, vinegar, honey, and a little cinnamon.

CHAPTER 24

Trial of the Cajack—Disappearance of Fritz—The Walrus—A
Storm—Anxieties Concerning Fritz—Saved!—
A Longer Expedition

The cajack had been ready to put to sea a long time, and Fritz, who had been appointed captain of it, was consumed by the desire to approve his title.

On the appointed day we all assembled upon the shore. Fritz desired to be solemnly invested with his command before embarking. Each of us, therefore, hastened to perform the office of valet, helping to dress and arm him for his expedition. Thus clad, our young Greenlander seized his paddle and harpoons, and cast a look of sublime defiance towards any invisible monsters of the deep that might be disposed to question his sovereignty of the seas. Then, like another Neptune, he installed himself in his vessel.

Assuming the requisite kneeling posture in the central opening of the cajack, he fastened his sea-dog-skin dress around the edge of it, so as to exclude the outer air, and, with his harpoons placed in their supports to the right and left of him, proceeded to inflate himself until he resembled in form a gigantic frog.

Ernest and Jack, with a strong rope, drew the vessel down the beach, while Francis pushed it behind; and Fritz set up a song of triumph on thus seeing himself abandoned to the mercy of the waves.

After riding at its ease upon the tranquil waters of our little bay for a few moments, the cajack began its trial evolutions. With the assistance of its paddle, Fritz first sent it swiftly ahead, cleaving the waters as it went. Then he inclined it to the right, then to the left. At last, to show that he could not be submerged, he completely capsized it, to the great fright of his mother and the great delight of his three brothers.

Fritz, excited beyond his wont by our plaudits, and not hearing the exclamations and appeals of his mother, who every moment expected some catastrophe, directed his vessel into the current at the mouth of Jackal River, which, before he had time to reconnoitre, carried him swiftly out into the open sea.

This imprudent act alarmed me. I embarked in all haste in the pirogue, and, accompanied by Jack and Ernest, set out in pursuit of the fugitive, praying my wife to have no fear, for that I should soon overtake Fritz, and would scold him roundly for his thoughtlessness.

By this time he had completely disappeared, and it was only by passing out of Deliverance Bay into the open sea that we could hope to discover his whereabouts.

Our canoe glided swiftly away, under the impulsion of our six oars, skimming over the waves like a sea-mew.

We were not long in reaching the shallows where the vessel which brought us to these parts had been wrecked, and where I supposed the current had carried my eldest son. There were sunken rocks there, and others which lifted their heads out of the sea, and upon these the waves broke heavily in foam and spray—portending, as I thought, rough weather.

In searching among the shallows for a place where we could rest in security upon our oars for a time, we found ourselves in a labyrinth of rocks, which completely shut out the horizon on all hands.

We wandered backwards and forwards in this species of archipelago for some time, unable to find a way out, but impatient to do so, in order to get sight of the dear, but imprudent, fugitive.

Suddenly, at a considerable distance, I saw a thin wreath of smoke curling upwards, followed, at the end of a second or two, by a feeble noise which I recognised as the far-off report of a gun.

"There is Fritz!" I cried, with a joyousness which it is impossible to set down in words.

"Where? where?" asked Ernest and Jack, looking impatiently in every direction.

At that same moment I heard another report like the first.

I fired one of my pistols, and it was replied to by a third report.

I assured my boys that Fritz was not more than a quarter of a league from us, and bade them lay on to their oars with a will.

A few minutes later we came up with the fugitive.

After Fritz had shown us a sea-cow, or sea-horse—as it is indifferently the custom to term the walrus—which he had just killed, and which lay dead upon a neighbouring fragment of rock, I gravely reproached him for the anxiety into which he had plunged all of us, and especially his mother, by his imprudence.

He excused himself by throwing all the blame upon the current, which he said had carried him away against his will. He passed by in silence any desire he might have had to try his cajack and his harpoons in the open sea.

I forgave him frankly, being only too happy to bring him safe and sound home to his mother; and, after removing from the walrus its head and tusks, as hunting ornaments for the cajack, we set out to return to port, Fritz leading the way.

On the voyage, Ernest asked me upon what I had based my calculation when, after the third report of Fritz's pistol, I had affirmed that he could not be more than a quarter of a league away.

"We are taught by the science of physics," I said, "that light travels at the rate of 186,000 miles a second. Sound, on the contrary, does not travel more than three hundred and fifty yards a second. Having counted three seconds between the time that I saw the smoke of Fritz's pistol and the time that I heard the report of it, I concluded that he must be something over a thousand yards away, and a thousand yards is about a quarter of a league."

"Has the same kind of calculation been applied to the light of the stars?" asked Ernest.

"Without doubt," I replied. "It takes eight minutes, seven seconds and a half for the light of the sun to reach the earth, and there exist fixed stars so far distant from us that it takes thousands of years for the light from them to reach us. If, for instance, one of them were suddenly to cease shining today, we should see its light for thousands of years to come."

"What an abyss is science!" said Ernest musingly; "and what a glorious thing it would be to know everything!"

In conversing in this wise, we had not travelled a third of the distance towards land when the storm which I expected, but did not think was so near, suddenly burst upon us with indescribable fury.

Unhappily Fritz was so far in advance of us that, what with the roaring of the winds and the waves, and the terrible torrents of rain which poured down from the overhanging clouds, we could give him no signal to come on board our safer craft. My heart was torn with an anguish which I will not attempt to describe. But I had to watch over the fate of others no less dear to me; and I ordered the boys to at once put on their swimming jackets and attach themselves to the canoe with straps, in order that, in case of our being capsized, they might not be carried away by the waves.

Moment by moment we feared that we should be swallowed up in the large abysses that opened beneath our frail craft. Moment by moment we found ourselves mounting with terror the glassy slopes of the enormous valleys that yawned before us.

The agonies of our own situation were as nothing compared to those I experienced concerning my unhappy son, who was the prime cause of our being brought into danger.

My heart suffered an age of anguish; but my lips were silent. I dared not alarm the two dear children of whom I still had charge, and who, perhaps, had fewer fears than I had, owing to the holy and ingenuous confidence with which my presence inspired them.

I was altogether lost in this painful train of thought, when, through the dread obscurity that surrounded us, and in spite of the mountainous waves that reared themselves on every hand, I perceived that we were near the entrance of Deliverance Bay.

I now took an oar myself, and we all worked with so much energy that in a few minutes we found ourselves in the wellknown avenue of rocks which, after our disastrous wreck upon the shallows we had just visited, led us to our deliverance long ago.

How can I express the ecstasy of joy with which I at length beheld upon the shore my wife and little Francis, and, above all, my dear boy Fritz, kneeling together and fervently praying that we might be restored to them out of the jaws of the great deep which seemed ready to swallow us up!

I shall not attempt to depict the overflowing joy with which we were received, nor that with which we ourselves once more embraced the dear ones whom we had hardly hoped to see again. My wife and I were so happy to see the children reunited, that we thought not for a moment of reproving Fritz for his disastrous imprudence.

This heavy and unexpected rain had so swollen the streams which poured down from among the rocks, that in several places, and especially at Falcon-nest, the floods were out and did damage which required immediate attention. Jackal River rose to so great a height that it almost carried away our bridge, and committed other ravages no less serious.

The reparation of these injuries, and divers other employments, such as salmon and sturgeon fishing (for which the season had again come round), occupied us for several days, and time flowed by so pleasantly that we well-nigh forgot the terror we had undergone during our adventure upon the open sea.

"Father," said Fritz at length, "my brothers and I have long had it in our minds to make another expedition, if we can get your consent.

We wish to visit Forest Grange and Prospect Hill, and to push our explorations both to the right and left of this route. What do you say?"

"If you wish it, my dear boys," I said, "I ask nothing better."

"In that case," said Fritz, "I will at once prepare some pemmican for the journey, if mamma will have the goodness to give me some pieces of bear's flesh."

"Pemmican!" said my wife. "What barbarous dish is that?"

"It is," said Fritz, "a preparation of bear's and deer's flesh, cut into small pieces and pounded into a lump, which the fur-dealers of Canada carry with them during their long excursions into the interior of their country. There is nothing like it for portability and nourishment combined. It is a very substantial food, and occupies a very small space."

Although my wife was less favourable than ever to excursions which removed her husband and the children from her, she, as usual, allowed herself to be persuaded of the necessity of the expedition, and even went so far as to assist Fritz in the preparation of the "barbarous dish."

While this was going on the other children busied themselves in preparing their arms and outfit, and, from their more than ordinary care and activity in the matter, I concluded that they placed a very high value upon the importance of the expedition they were about to undertake.

The old truck, turned into a wagon by the addition of a couple of cannon-wheels, was loaded with bags and baskets of all kinds, with the tent, and with the cajack.

Master Jack, thinking he was not seen by me, added a few pigeons to our supply of pemmican, with the object, I suppose, of varying his food a little when he grew tired of pounded bear's flesh.

I affected not to be conscious of the innocent trick, and hastened the preparations for our departure.

CHAPTER 25

Expedition to Forest Grange—The Hyena—The Carrier-Pigeon—
Fritz's Letter—The Black Swan—The Royal Heron—More Ravages
by Monkeys—How They Were Punished—Serious Devastation
by Huge Beasts

On the morning of the day fixed for the setting out of the expedition, my wife declined, much to my surprise, to take part in it, saying that she preferred repose for a time. Ernest also, after many warm discussions with his brothers, declared that he was equally in need of rest, and should stay at home with his mother.

Seeing our project thus modified, I determined to let the three boys undertake the expedition alone while I remained at Rockhouse, and, with the assistance of Ernest, tried my hand at the construction of a sugar-press.

Our three young hunters made their adieux, and set out gaily, with a notable provision of good wishes, exhortations, councils, and advice.

After leaving us they pushed swiftly on to Forest Grange, where they had determined to remain during the first and following days.

On approaching the farmery they were not a little surprised to hear a succession of short and sharp bursts of what seemed to be human laughter. Their oxen and their dogs showed considerable alarm; while Jack's ostrich, a creature singularly impressionable—I might almost say very nervous by nature—took fright and bolted with its young rider, on its back, in the direction of Forest Grange River.

Fritz and his brother dismounted to discover the cause of this panic; and while the former tried to calm the terror of the animals, the latter advanced cautiously through the copse to take further observations. He was simply to do this, his brother instructing him to return at once in case of encountering any peril.

Little Francis, although much daunted by the terrible laughter which still broke forth from time to time, pushed on with stealthy steps. His gun was held in readiness to fire, and in a low voice he encouraged the dogs, who seemed but little disposed to follow him.

In the course of a few minutes, on softly pulling aside a bush, he saw, some eighty paces ahead of him, a huge hyena in the act of devouring a ram which it had just killed.

Francis, although he fully comprehended the risk of the act, did not hesitate to at once fire at the beast. His ball smashed one of its fore-feet and passed thence into its chest, leaving a large gaping wound.

Fritz, after having succeeded—but not without considerable trouble—in restraining the backward course of the oxen, fastened them securely to a couple of trees, and hastened to the help of his brother, who, however, had now no need of his assistance.

The two dogs, who from a state of the most incomprehensible timidity had passed to a condition of extreme fury, had flung themselves upon the prostrate enemy.

Fritz, therefore, dared not fire for fear of shooting Fawn or Brown, who, happily, in a short time made themselves masters of the field of battle. Though the hyena was dead, and they had torn from him his prey, they still stood over him menacingly, ears erect, teeth displayed, and eyes sparkling with malice.

The three boys then set out for Forest Grange, carrying their booty with them upon the truck. They resolved to skin the beast during their sojourn at the farmery.

We who remained at Rock-house, while sitting under the sheltering foliage of the verandah when the labours of the day were ended, found little else to talk about beyond the probable course taken by the three adventurous young travellers.

"What is that?" I exclaimed, as something flew past me. "It is a belated pigeon, I suppose, entering the dove-cot. I wonder where it has been. It is too dark to see whether it is one of our own brood or a stranger which has mistaken its roosting-place."

"Shut down the trap! shut down the trap!" cried Ernest excitedly. "Who knows but it may be a carrier with news from Sydney? Were you not speaking today, father, of the likelihood of our being in the neighbourhood of the colony of which that is the capital? If the pigeon which has just entered should really turn out to be a courier thence, we might use it to open up a correspondence with New South Wales."

"I could heartily desire that it might be so, my dear child," I replied sadly; "but it would be without the remotest hope that the desire would be realised. But it grows late; let us to bed. The first thing tomorrow morning, you can, if you so wish it, go and consult your good courier from Sydney, and read to us the news which you hope to find under its wing. In the meantime do not dream too wildly while you are asleep tonight."

The next morning, rising much earlier than was usual with him, Ernest went out to the dove-cot, and afterwards spent some time in the library.

As his mother and I were sitting down to breakfast, we saw him coming gravely towards us, bowing as he approached. Then, with an air of mock dignity, he presented us with a paper, folded and sealed in the form of a government despatch.

"To you, most noble owners of this domain," he said, "the humble Postmaster of Rock-house presents his respectful compliments, and begs that you will not too severely condemn him for delaying until now to present you with the despatches from Forest Grange and Sydney. The post arrived last night, but, owing to circumstances beyond his own control, your devoted servant was not permitted to open the bag until this morning."

Deliberately unfolding his paper, Ernest again saluted us, and in a clear measured voice proceeded to read as follows:

" 'THE GOVERNOR-GENERAL OF NEW SOUTH WALES, TO HIS EXCELLENCY THE GOVERNOR OF ROCK-HOUSE, FALCON-NEST, UNDER-TENT, FOREST GRANGE, SUGAR-CANE GROVE, &C. &C., GREETING.

" 'Most noble, well-beloved, and trusty Ally,

" 'We learn, with high displeasure, that within the week last past, to wit, this morning, three disreputable adventurers have set out from your Colony with the object and intention of living by brigandage, to the no small hurt and detriment of the game, large and small, of this Province.

" 'We learn also that a ferocious troop of hyenas, as destructive to property as they are dangerous to human life, have recently made an irruption into a certain portion of the territory under your Government, to wit, that portion of it known by the name and style of Forest Grange, and have already caused considerable damage to the flocks and herds depasturing thereabouts.

" 'In consequence, we pray you to advise yourself speedily of some means whereby these disorders may be promptly suppressed, and to take measures both for the arrest and return of the fugitive brigands, and for maintaining the legal rights of man and the domestic animals, as against the ravages of wild beasts.

"'Accept, most noble, well-beloved, and trusty Ally, the assurance of my highest consideration and esteem.

"'Given at Sydney, New South Wales, this 12th of the present month, in the years 34 of the Colony.

"'(Signed) PHILLIP PHILLIPSON,

"'GOVERNOR.'"

His reading achieved, Ernest burst into loud laughter, and began dancing so wildly that a small note escaped from his pocket and fell to the ground. I ran to pick it up, but Ernest was before me.

"This," said he, "is a private letter from Forest Grange. Nevertheless, if you desire it, I will give your highnesses the contents of it. It may not be so pompously nor so elegantly worded, perhaps, but I fancy it contains more truth than the official despatch of the good Sir Phillip Phillipson, who, so far as I can judge, seems to have lent too ready an ear to mere exaggerated rumours concerning the condition of this colony."

"You are giving us a strange enigma to solve," I said. "Did Fritz, before he set out, hand you a letter for me with instructions not to deliver it till he was far upon his journey? Because if——"

"No, dear father," replied Ernest, who saw that his mother was growing anxious. "The truth is, that this note which I hold in my hand was brought last night by the belated pigeon that you saw enter the dove-cot, and I should have read it to you last night had I been able to get at it in the dark. These are the contents of it, word for word:

"'Well-beloved Parents and dear Ernest,

"'An enormous hyena killed two of our lambs and a ram. Francis behaved gloriously. He knocked it over with a shot which struck it full in the breast. The dogs finished it. We have passed the remainder of the day skinning it. It is a magnificent skin. Our pemmican is wretched stuff. Mother was quite right in showing her contempt of my new-fangled cookery.

"'Yours affectionately,

"'FRITZ.

"'Forest Grange, the 12th instant.'"

"A true hunter's letter!" I said, laughing. "And heaven be praised that my little Francis was able to achieve so easy a victory over this terrible enemy!"

Towards sunset, a little later than on the previous evening, a second carrier-pigeon entered the dove-cot.

Ernest at once caught it, and brought us the following note:

"All well during the night. Splendid morning. A cruise on Forest Grange Lake in the cajack. Capture of black swan, royal heron, cranes, and black diver-ducks. To Prospect Hill to-morrow.

"Adieu to all.

"FRITZ, JACK, FRANCIS."

This note reassured us. It showed, at all events, that no other hyena had put in an appearance. As to its enigmatical details, they were explained fully by the young adventurers after the expedition.

In setting out upon his explorations, Fritz had determined, if possible, to take some black swans alive. Arming himself, therefore, with a long bamboo, furnished at its ends with a wire noose, he contrived to approach three young ones of the species, which, being less wild than the older ones, suffered themselves to be taken without much trouble. Brought living to Rock-house, the feathered prisoners, with their shining black plumage and brilliant red beaks, became handsome ornaments to the glassy waters of Deliverance Bay.

Scarcely had the black swans been secured, when a royal heron made its way out of the reeds. Fritz at once cast a lasso, which caught his prey by the neck. The noble bird made a desperate struggle to escape, flapping its wings, kicking with its long legs, and endeavouring to break asunder the rope with its beak. So great was its strength, that Fritz had to run his cajack aground before he could take it. Once unable to draw the boat after it, the bird fell half strangled and became an easy prey to the determined young hunter. Tying its wings and legs, and bandaging its eyes, he brought it home alive.

The dinner hour found all three of the brothers reassembled, and talking of their several exploits. They dined with the best possible appetite off a peccary ham, potatoes roasted among the embers of a wood fire, the fruit of the guava, and some cinnamon apples. As to the pemmican, they found it so little to their taste that they gave it to the dogs, who enjoyed it immensely.

I shall here transcribe, as nearly as possible in his own words, the account Fritz gave us of the journey he made with his brothers to the hut at Prospect Hill, which they reached at noon on the day after their exploration of the lake.

"Scarcely had we entered the little pine-wood," said he, "when we were furiously attacked by a horde of monkeys, who sat among the branches of the trees, chattering, grinding their teeth, and literally raining down pine-cones upon us. Although the fruit was for the most part ripe, the quantity of it became very embarrassing, and in order to put an end to the attack, we fired a few shots at random. To our great regret, four or five of our aggressors fell dead at our feet. Their numerous comrades, justly alarmed at our method of rewarding their ill-timed pleasantries, became immediately silent and invisible.

"In passing through Sugar-cane Grove, I was astonished to find that the new growth, which had reached a height of eight or ten feet, was beaten down and broken as if a fierce storm of hail had fallen upon it.

"At length we got to Prospect Hill, where, after attending to our beasts and unloading our spoils, we made an inspection of the place. You will be sorry to hear it, dear father, but not more sorry than I am to have it to tell—the abominable monkeys have committed even worse ravages here than they did at Forest Grange: everything is laid waste; we even had to rebuild the little hut before we could inhabit it for the night.

"Before we set out we had feared something of the kind, and were prepared to visit the monkeys with condign punishment. To that end we, in the evening, filled a number of gourd-vessels and cocoa-nut shells with fresh goat's milk, palm-tree wine, and pounded millet. Into each of them we poured a few drops of a poisonous drug which Ernest had prepared for us, at my request, and which we carried in a gourd-bottle. This done, we hung our deadly chalices to the branches of the neighbouring trees, and went to bed upon our bags of cotton.

"In spite of our fatigue, we found it almost impossible to sleep. At first we were disturbed by the cries of strange animals and the barking of our dogs, and then by the invasion of monkeys, who, however, soon found out and lapped up with avidity the choice repast we had prepared for them.

"At daybreak the next morning, curious to know what had passed during the night, we got up and went abroad. We were astonished to witness the effects of our essay in toxicology. You may rest quite satisfied: I will undertake to say that there is not a living monkey remaining for two leagues round Prospect Hill. Nor do I think it likely that a fresh colony will establish itself to partake of the feast with which we are prepared to provide them. Seeing the terrible destruction the monkeys had wrought, we did not think you would reprove us for our wholesale slaughter, which I assure you left no traces whatever upon our own consciences.

"It was now that we sent you our third carrier-pigeon, with a despatch penned by Jack in a style pompous and altogether Oriental, giving you an account of our grotesque expedition, and at the same time news of our intended return."

The letter of which Fritz spoke just above quite reassured us as to the safety of our three young hunters. But shortly after dinner on the fourth day, a fourth carrier-pigeon arrived, bringing the following letter:

"The defile is forced. As far as Sugar-cane Grove everything is laid waste. The new growth of sugar is pulled up, broken down, trampled upon, destroyed. Numberless and enormous footprints of huge beasts are seen in the soil. Hasten, dear father, to our help. We dare not go forward nor retire; and although quite safe at present, we know not how to prepare for a danger of which we know not the gravity nor the quarter from which it may menace us."

This news was of a totally different character from any that had preceded it, and you may be sure I did not waste time in idle comments upon it.

Without the least delay, I saddled the onager, and, telling my wife and Ernest to follow me next day to the defile, I set out at a gallop.

CHAPTER 26

Construction of a Summer Residence—The Fruits of the Cacao and Banana Trees—The Mysterious Sack—The Sultan Fowl—Restoration of Falcon-nest—Fortification of Shark Island

I accomplished in three hours a journey which ordinarily occupied six. My prompt arrival, upon which my boys had hardly ventured to count—not knowing whether the carrier-pigeon had reached us—was hailed with shouts of joy and warm embraces.

Devastation met my gaze on every hand. The posts which had served to close the narrow defile between the rocks, and which we had been at so much trouble to place there, lay trampled into the soil, snapped off at the base like so many dry reeds. A neighbouring grove of trees, which we had begun to train in such a manner that they would, in the course of a few months, form a sort of Kamskatka cabin for our summer residence during the heat of the season, were torn down by the branches, and completely ruined. In the bamboo plantation all the young plants were either trampled down or devoured. But the worst part of the devastation was apparent in Sugar-cane Grove. Those of our plants which were not hopelessly trodden under foot were either broken to pieces or half-eaten. There was nothing, even down to the hut we had used for curing flesh, which did not bear marks of the prevailing ruin.

We hastily erected the tent, and got together a large quantity of wood, with which we lighted fires to protect ourselves against the attacks of wild beasts during the darkness. As you may conceive, we did not pass a very tranquil night. Fritz and I, gun in hand and ears and eyes on the alert, sat up till daylight, awaiting whatever danger might present itself.

The next day, towards noon, Ernest and his mother arrived upon the cow and the ass, which were well laden with baggage, and we prepared for a lengthy sojourn in the neighbourhood. I intended, indeed, to repair all the damage that had been done, so as once more to leave everything in security.

When the re-fortification of the defile had been completed—an undertaking which occupied us for a week—I set about constructing a summer residence, after the Kamskatka fashion. I chose four fine trees whose branches interlaced each other at a height of about twenty feet from the ground, and across these branches I laid a floor. The foliage formed the side walls and the roof. I devised a ladder which, while strong and convenient both for ascent and descent, could be lifted up upon the floor whenever we pleased. The aerial cabin finished, it presented a highly picturesque appearance, and served at once for a sleeping chamber, an observatory, and a fowl-house. We were henceforth in no fear about our Prospect Hill colony of poultry.

This new dwelling was unanimously called the Hermitage.

The labours I have mentioned were not our sole occupation during this period. While I was at work upon the Hermitage, and my wife was employed in her domestic duties, which were neither light nor unimportant, the boys made several excursions, each time bringing home some novel kind of booty.

For instance, Fritz returned from one of his later journeys, bringing with him two kinds of fruit which he had taken for gherkins or young cucumbers, but which in reality were the fruits of the cacao and banana trees. We tasted both, and I am bound to say that neither of them came up to its reputation in point of delicacy. The pips of the cacao, buried like those of the apple in a sort of insipidly-sweet pap, were exquisitely bitter. The banana fruit was hardly agreeable: it had a neutral kind of flavour on the palate, something like half-rotten pears.

"It is very strange," I said, "that these fruits, so highly prized elsewhere, should seem to us to have a flavour so disagreeable. In the West Indies, the pulp of the cacao, well sprinkled with sugar, is held in the highest esteem, while its pips, which we find so bitter, are dried to form chocolate, pounded with sugar, and pronounced delicious. In both the Indies the fruit of the banana, whether roasted or boiled, is found to be extraordinarily agreeable to the taste. Perhaps it is because it is gathered at some particular period—before it is ripe, maybe."

"If that is the case," said my wife, "I will take possession of some of these fruits and plant them in my garden. I hope that, by this means, we shall be able to find them as delicious as other people."

"Be careful then, my dear," I said, "to set the pips of the cacao in well-watered soil, and do it the moment you take them out of the pulp in which they are embedded, otherwise they will not grow. As to the bananas, they are usually reproduced by slips. If you wish it, Fritz shall get you some, and also some more cacao fruit."

Accordingly, on the day before that appointed for our return to Rock-house, Fritz received a commission from his mother to supply her both with banana slips and cacao fruit, and from me to seek, during this last excursion of the present expedition, as many new specimens as he could find both of the animal and the vegetable kingdoms.

He set out on the river in his cajack, towing behind him a kind of Californian raft, very light but very strong. It returned in the evening laden almost to sinking point.

Jack, Ernest, and Francis ran to assist him in unloading the cargo of the little flotilla, and dividing the spoils among them, carried them up the bank to the cabin. Ernest and Francis had already set out with their loads, when Fritz, saying, "Here is something for you," handed over to Jack a large wet sack, in which singular movements and noises manifested themselves.

Jack hid himself behind a bush and opened the bag. At sight of its contents he uttered an exclamation of surprise, and executed a joy-dance. Then, thanking his brother for his present, he carried the sack along the bank of the river, and placed it half in the water and half out, in a retired spot where he could find it next morning.

Fritz leapt to land with a great bird, whose legs and wings were tied and its eyes bandaged, and presented it to us with an air of supreme satisfaction. It was a fine Sultan fowl.

We had none of us been idle during his absence. We had prepared everything for our departure on the following day.

We made the journey to Rock-house without misadventure. Jack, mounted upon his ostrich, went on before us, and took advantage of the opportunity thus afforded him to deposit in the soft mud of Goose Marsh the mysterious sack which his brother had given him on the preceding evening.

Soon after the arrival of Fritz, who paddled in about two hours before sundown, we sat down to a comfortable repast.

Dinner over, we were seated under the verandah of the grotto, chattering peacefully as our custom was, when we were startled by the roaring of some strange animal. The noise at first sounded like distant thunder. It came from the neighbourhood of Goose Marsh.

Fritz, who in such cases was usually the first to fly to arms, did not move from his seat, but sat smiling in a manner that almost reassured me.

"Do not alarm yourselves, my dears," I said; "I dare say that which we have so readily taken for a wild beast is nothing more than a bittern or marsh-pig."

"At all events," said Fritz, "it may only be a small serenade given in our honour by Jack's giant frog."

"Ho, ho!" replied I, laughing; "so it is a trick that young giddy-head is playing us, is it? I can understand now all about the mysterious sack: it was used, I presume, to carry this huge frog home."

A few days afterwards, when we had recovered a little from the fatigue attendant on our last expedition, my wife urged me to repair our old dwelling at Falcon-nest.

Thenceforward the restoration of what we were now pleased to call Fig-tree Castle proceeded with rapidity. The arched roots at the base were planed up and polished, and the terrace on the top of them was relaid with loam, and made impervious to the wet with a coating of tar and resin. The house in the branches was roofed with bark, carefully closed at the joints, while the flooring around it was garnished with a balcony of trellis-work, which gave it a very picturesque appearance. In short, our old nest, unsightly and ill-contrived as it was at first, now became, thanks to our improved skill in carpentry, a very charming-looking and very comfortable dwelling.

This, so to speak, was but a labour of pleasure. Fritz was for doing something more useful. To that end he determined to fortify Shark Island.

The enterprise was a difficult one, but we achieved it without any great expenditure of time or any overwhelming fatigue. I began by constructing a winch upon the upper rocks, with the view of placing our four cannon there. This done, we set to work to raise the guns. As the height was between fifty and sixty feet, and the ordnance was heavy, you may be sure this was no light labour. However, we accomplished it without accident.

Behind the cannon, which were mounted upon their carriages and pointed towards the sea, we built a sort of watch-tower with planks and bamboo-canes; and, hard by, raised a mast, with running cordage attached, for the hoisting of signal-flags. These were to be white in times of tranquillity, and red when we apprehended danger.

The restoration of Falcon-nest and the fortification of Shark Island took us about two months, and when we had finished we determined to celebrate the event.

We fired off six rounds of ordnance as a grand salute, and for the first time hoisted the Swiss flag over our dominions.

CHAPTER 27

Condition of the Colony at the End of Ten Years—Excursion by Fritz in the Cajack—Pearl Bay—The Dog-Fish—The Albatross

Chapter has added itself to chapter as year has added itself to year since I began to narrate the history of my life, or rather that of my family, during the decade that we have lived upon this lonely island.

During these ten years what undertakings, small and great, have we not achieved? What events, trivial and serious, have not occurred in our midst? Each day has brought with it its labours and its anxieties; each day has also brought with it its rewards and its pleasures.

Putting aside a few inevitable failures and vexations, putting aside also a few passing attacks of sickness, equally inevitable, everything had grown around us—our trees, our gardens, our cattle and poultry, our children, and our love. The eaglets had become eagles. All four of our boys, as it appeared to me, had grown as handsome as they were good, each following the peculiarities of his own humour and temperament. They loved each other tenderly, with an affection at once manly and child-like. They worked like strong men and played like boys. Fritz had attained his twenty-fourth year, Ernest his twenty-second, Jack his twentieth, and Francis his seventeenth.

Time had laid the lightest touch upon the features of my beloved wife, who still remained, as she always had been, the angel of our solitude. Her pure soul shone youthful as ever through the sweet expression of her countenance. The children adored her, and loaded her with tendernesses. Each strove to outdo the other in anticipating her lightest wish, in sparing her an unnecessary anxiety, in giving her an unexpected pleasure, in doing her will upon the slightest hint.

Our animals, who were our companions and friends, had prospered as we had. Grumbler had achieved his full growth. The cow had presented us with a calf yearly, and of her numerous progeny we had spared two, one of which had become a fine milch cow, and the other a powerful bull. We called the first Swan, because of the whiteness of her coat; and the second Roarer, because of his terrible voice.

We had also added to our stock two young asses—a male and a female—one of which we christened Arrow, and the other Sprightly. Lastly, we had saved out of the far too numerous offspring of the agile jackal a specimen which promised to become an excellent hunter, and to which Jack had given the grotesque name of Cocoa.

One day, when Fritz, unknown to us, had set out early in the morning in his cajack, we went in the afternoon to the fortifications on Shark Island, to endeavour to get a sight, if possible, of the adventurer. The white flag floated from the top of the mast; the cannon lay loaded and ready to speak, at the word of command, with their formidable throats.

We waited some time without being able to see anything of our runaway. At last, by the aid of the telescope, I perceived a black speck on the water. It speedily assumed larger dimensions, and at last a definite shape. It was Fritz. His paddle dipped regularly in the tranquil mirror of the sea, but, as far as I could judge, much more slowly than usual. He was making his course towards Deliverance Bay.

We fired the cannon and greeted our sailor with loud hurrahs. Then we descended in all haste to receive him as he landed near Rock-house.

At the prow of the canoe—that is to say, at the point where we had fixed the head of the walrus, was suspended a large bundle of what appeared to be stout thorny feathers. It was, in point of fact, a new supply of the gelatinous sea-weed of which my wife made jelly. At the poop hung a large sack well filled, half in the water and half out. At one side of the cajack floated an important capture, the nature of which we could not quite make out.

The cajack having been drawn up on the beach and unloaded, we surrounded Fritz to hear the story of the voyage, which, on his part, he was only too ready to recount.

"First of all, dear father," he said, "I have to beg your forgiveness for setting out this morning without obtaining your leave to do so. Having a craft so light and so altogether suitable, I could not resist a desire that sometimes comes over me to make a voyage in it. I have for a long time wished to become better acquainted with the coast west of Deliverance Bay, and also to explore the part where I killed the walrus. If you had forbidden me I should not have disobeyed you, and it was because I feared you might have forbidden me, on account of the supposed danger of the cruise, that I set out without your knowledge. To provide against unforeseen exigencies, which might have prolonged my journey, I took with me, besides provisions, a boathook, a harpoon, some fishing-lines, my axe, my gun, my pistol, a compass, and my eagle.

"The weather was everything I could have desired. The sea was calm and the sky cloudless. I took advantage of a few minutes when you were engaged in the grotto, to jump into my cajack and pull into the river current, which in a very short time carried me out of your sight. On reaching the spot where ten years ago our vessel was wrecked, I found the water so clear that I could see on the smooth sandy bottom several cannon, a quantity of shot, a number of bars of iron, and other objects, which we shall do well to get up when you have made the diving-bell you were talking about the other day.

"I continued my voyage, and, when I passed the rocky vault, found myself in a magnificent bay from the shore of which a splendid savannah stretched away till it was lost to view on the horizon. Here and there clumps of verdant foliage sprang from the clefts of the rocks, while into the centre of the bay poured a large river whose banks were lined with magnificent cedar-trees.

"In cruising round the coast of this bay I perceived in the depths of the water, which was transparent as crystal, millions of shell-fish that seemed to be tied together and fastened to their shells by numberless filaments, which looked like tufts of hair. Thinking that these fish would probably be more agreeable to the taste than the oysters which we take in Deliverance Bay, I detached some with my boathook and fished them up with my lines. I threw upon the beach those which I intended to eat, and put the rest into a sack, which I tied to the stern of my canoe, in order to bring a few home to you. Then I landed to take a rest. On opening my oysters, which appeared to be very tough, I found in them several little round bodies of the size of peas, very brilliant, and resembling pearls. I leave you to judge whether I am right in my conjecture. There they are—examine them."

At these words, Ernest, Jack, and Francis hastened to look at the shells which Fritz handed to me. Our brave adventurer was right: the small round bodies of which he had spoken were indeed pearls of a dazzling whiteness, and of rare purity and fineness. Many of them were unusually large.

"You have found a real treasure, my dear Fritz," I replied. "Whole nations would envy you your discovery, for a pearl-bank such as you describe is a mine worth millions. Unhappily, it is impossible for us to profit by it, or even to make a market out of sea-swallows' nests, for sea-swallows they are. We have no relations with the rest of the world, and for our own use these inestimable treasures are not worth nearly so much as a bag of nails or a measure of wheat. Nevertheless, as it would be ungrateful to neglect the gifts which Providence throws in our way, and as we may be permitted some day to join our friends in Europe, we will make an early expedition to this opulent bay. For who knows but the seemingly useless labours of the present time may in the future contribute to the well-being of all of us? Now, my dear son, continue your narrative."

Fritz proceeded:

"After replenishing my stock of fresh water, I set out again, and soon reached the promontory which shuts in Pearl Bay. It faces Sea-gull Arch, and is distant from it about a league. There is a long ridge of sunken rocks, which completely separates the bay from the open sea, except in one part, where there is a deep clear channel, somewhat narrow but very convenient. It would be impossible to find a situation more advantageous for a seaport.

"As I was making my way through this sea-pass, an unexpected current brought me to a sudden standstill, and I was obliged to coast along the promontory to find an opening similar to that by which I had entered on the other side. But I did not succeed. On my way I saw an immense number of marine animals of the size and shape of dog-fish, playing upon the rocks and in the water, and leaping from the one to the other in turns. I was too far off to draw upon them, but I nevertheless had a strong desire to make their acquaintance. I therefore rowed a little nearer, and put up my eagle, which swiftly pounced down in the midst of the thoughtless shoal. Quitting my canoe, I leapt from rock to rock, and arrived just in time to seize the prey, which the eagle was already rending. The entire shoal had disappeared as if by enchantment."

"But," I asked, "how did you manage to bring your booty home? It must be very heavy."

"That consideration gave me some trouble," replied Fritz. "I did not like to leave my dog-fish behind at any cost; and yet I knew that, unless I could hit upon some means of lightening its weight a good deal, it would be impossible to bring it with me. While casting about for a plan, I was struck by the enormous quantity of sea-birds that were circling and screaming around me. There were sea-swallows, mews, gulls, petrels, albatrosses, and several other kinds unknown to me. Their noise became so insupportable that, to rid myself of them, I hit out wildly with my boat-hook. One fell at my feet stunned, and lay there with wide-extended wings. It was a kind of albatross, which I believe is called by sailors the frigate bird.

"Remembering then a device in use among the Greenlanders, I pulled out one of the bird's largest feathers, and used it as a pipe to inflate my dog-fish. In this state I tied the creature to the side of my cajack, and it rode buoyantly upon the sea. But it was time now to think of returning, and I stopped no more.

"I found my way out of the labyrinth of rocks in safety, and laying on upon my paddle soon found myself in known waters.

"There I saw our white flag floating in the breeze afar off, and heard the welcome report of our artillery."

CHAPTER 28

A Confidential Conversation with Fritz—The English Girl on the Burning Rock—A Pearl-Fishing Expedition—Cape Flat-nose—Pearl-Fishing—The Return

So far Fritz had ended his narrative. But while his mother and brothers were examining with much curiosity the spoils he had brought home, he took me mysteriously on one side and led me to a distant bank, upon which we sat down. He there completed his account as follows:—

"I have not told you all, dear father," he said. "The strangest part of the story remains at present for your ear alone. As I was searching over the albatross which I knocked down, to select a feather suitable for my purpose, I found a piece of linen rag tied to one of its legs. I at once detached it, and saw written upon it in English, in a kind of red ink, these strange words:—

"*'Whoever you may be to whom God bears this message from an unfortunate girl, seek out a volcanic island, which you will recognize by the flame that rises from one of its craters. Save the unhappy lost one of the Burning Rock!'*

"Amazed, I read and re-read the message a half-score times, to assure myself that I was not dreaming. 'What!' I cried, 'is it possible—a human being living in these uninhabited parts? How came she here? Without doubt like we did, by shipwreck. Oh, that I may be able to find her in time to save her life!'

"Thereupon I endeavoured to revive the poor bird, which happily was only stunned. I poured a drop of hydromel into its beak, and it seemed to be recovering. Then with a feather dipped in the bleeding wound of the dog-fish, I wrote in English upon a piece of my handkerchief:

"*'Have faith in God. In all probability succour is near.'*

"I tied the two pieces of rag to the leg of the albatross, now completely recovered from its swoon, and allowed it to try its wings.

It at once flew off to the westward with a swiftness that vexed me not a little, for I had hoped that it would go at a slower pace, and thus enable me to follow it, and discover the Burning Rock.

"This is what I wanted to tell you alone, father. And now, think you that my message of comfort has reached the poor unfortunate who yearns for it? Where is she? How can I find her?"

"My dear son," I replied, "I rejoice extremely in the prudence with which you have conducted this matter, and I congratulate you upon it. You did well to reserve your account of it for my ear alone, because in divulging it to your mother and brothers you would have caused them an amount of anxiety which it was your duty, as a son and a brother, to spare them. It may unhappily be the case that the message you found tied to the leg of the albatross is an old one written many months since. It may also be that the unfortunate whom you desire to save is separated from us by a wide tract of ocean; for the albatross is a powerful bird upon the wing, and traverses inconceivable distances in a few days. The country whence it came, and to which it has probably returned, may therefore be leagues away from our colony. However, we will speak of that later on. For the present, let us return to the family, who will wonder what business we have on hand to hold us in this mysterious converse."

Our conversation during the meal turned naturally upon the pearl-oyster, and I was compelled to describe the manner in which the gem forms itself in the shell, the method of fishing, the devices of the divers, the dangers to which they are subject, and so on.

These points settled, we decided that, having so inexhaustible a mine of wealth in the immediate neighbourhood, it was our duty to possess ourselves of some of its riches as soon as possible. We had, however, no implements suitable to oyster-fishing, and it became necessary that each of us should set to work to make some. I myself forged four iron hooks, two large and two small, which were intended to be hung to the bottom of the canoe in such wise that they would drag the bottom, and bring our prey to the surface. Francis assisted his mother in making some landing-nets, to get them ashore when brought there. Ernest employed himself in making, after a design I had given him, a long instrument that would serve to detach the nests of the sea-swallows; while Jack, having the same end in view, knotted a rope and fastened a hook to it, with the intention of climbing where Ernest would only venture to reach with a pole.

These preparations made, we got ready to set out on our voyage. Our provisions were varied and plentiful—fresh pemmican, made on an improved plan since Fritz's failure six or seven years ago, cassava cakes, maize, almonds, and a small cask of hydromel. These, with our arms and baggage, were placed on board the pirogue, and on an early day, when the weather was favourable, we set sail, leaving my wife at home under the care of Francis.

Arrived at length in the tranquil waters of a large bay, we saw, playing upon its smooth surface, as upon a mirror, a large quantity of the elegant shell-fish known as argonauta, or nautili. Our pilots possessed themselves of some fine specimens, which were carefully laid away in the pirogue.

Soon afterwards we reached a promontory which looked as if it had been crushed in by a blow, from which circumstance we at once named it Cape Flat-nose. When we had doubled it we saw in the distance, through Rock Arch, the famous object of our search —Pearl Bay.

The gigantic vault, under which we passed, merited all the praises which Fritz had bestowed on it. Like him, we were assailed on reaching it by myriads of sea-swallows, which circled round, and rose and fell on every side of us, like gnats on a summer evening.

As you may imagine, we wasted no time in admiration, but set to work at once upon the nests nearest at hand. Jack's knotted rope was of the first utility to reach the juttings of the rocks; but as the adventurous spirits of my sons carried them beyond the bounds of prudence, I was obliged to order them to desist from their harvest. Our booty was placed in the pirogue, and, after partaking of some refreshment, we again set out upon our voyage.

The rising tide helped us, without misadventure, through the dangerous defile of sunken rocks of which Fritz had told us, and before long we found ourselves in one of the most magnificent bays I had ever seen. It was about six or eight leagues in circuit. Several small islands, scattered about its surface, rendered it the more picturesque in appearance. It was shut in from the sea by a belt of broken rocks, in the centre of which was a defile of some fathoms in width, offering a commodious entrance to the largest vessels. The only objection a sailor could have had to it was that here and there it was dotted with sandbanks and shallows; but these latter, being partly composed of oyster-beds rising to the level of the water, were easily seen and consequently not very dangerous.

It was with a sensation of vivid delight that we found ourselves floating over this beautiful sheet of water; and, as we coasted round its shore, the verdant prairies beyond it, the shadowy woods, the undulating hills, and the picturesque river, gave pleasure to our eyes, and seemed to put hope into our hearts. A creek a few paces from the bank of pearl-oysters was chosen for a landing-place. Our dogs, to whom we had doled out water sparingly during the passage, waited not for our invitation to leap over the side of the pirogue and make for a small clear stream, running into the bay, to slake their thirst.

We were not long in following the example of our animals. The day was declining, and the first thing to be done on landing was to prepare our supper and provide a lodging for the night. We were not long in improvising a repast. It consisted of pemmican soup, boiled potatoes, and maize-cakes.

A great fire was lighted with waifs and strays washed up during the course of ages by the sea, and dried in the sun. Our dogs were left on the beach. We ourselves slept on board the pirogue, which was anchored in the creek, and upon the deck of which we had set up our tent.

CHAPTER 29

The Lions—Death of Fan—Fritz's Expedition—The Spermaceti Whale

At daybreak we were all afoot, and, after a good repast, proceeded to the pearl-bank, where the supply was so abundant that I determined to stay three days. Our plan was to take our oysters and spread them out upon the sand, where the sun speedily opened them for us, and leave them to putrefy; after which, as I had read, we could take our pearls easily. While thus employed, we lighted upon two kinds of soda among the rocks. With one of them I hoped to make a better kind of soap than we had hitherto been using, while with the other I thought I should be able to purify our sugar.

Each evening, about an hour before preparing our supper, it was our custom to make a pedestrian excursion into the savannah, whence we brought in specimens of rare vegetables or birds.

On the evening of the third day we lighted our fires upon the beach as usual, and, as everything seemed tranquil, were about to retire to rest, when we were startled by a succession of loud roarings which, proceeding from the depths of the forest, were re-echoed by the distant mountains.

In a few moments, by the lurid glare of our fires, we saw a beast of enormous size approaching with a lithe and stately tread.

It was a lion.

On arriving in front of the pile of glowing timber, he came to a dead stand. The flame lighted up his face, in which we read power, fierceness, and hunger. He lashed his tawny flanks furiously with his tail, and looked as if he were about to spring upon us. This fearful pantomime lasted for some time. We dared not move, and I was reflecting whether it would even be wise to fire, when we heard the report of a gun.

"It is Fritz!" said Ernest in a voice trembling with fear.

The lion leapt up, uttering a roar of pain, and fell fainting in a stream of blood that poured from its huge breast.

"We are saved!" I cried. "We are saved! The lion has been pierced to the heart! Fritz is a dead shot indeed!"

I drew up the anchor, and with a few strokes of the oar brought myself near enough to the beach to leap ashore.

I advised Ernest and Jack to remain where they were.

The dogs came bounding up to lick my hand, but in a moment began to howl again, and directed my attention towards the wood. It was a notification not to be disregarded.

I at once paused, and it was well I did, for at the same instant there emerged from the darkness of the forest a huge lioness—the female, no doubt, of the superb animal Fritz had just killed.

The lioness, by her hoarse purrings, seemed to be calling her companion. Becoming suspicious that all was not well with him, she began sniffing on all sides, and lashing her flanks with her tail as if in the deepest anguish. Presently she caught sight of the corpse. She hastened towards it, and tenderly licked the still bleeding wound. Then, comprehending that her companion was in truth dead, she uttered a terrible roar, ground her teeth fiercely, and, her eyes flaming with vengeance, peered into the surrounding darkness as if seeking a victim to offer up as a sacrifice to her combined rage and despair.

At this moment the report of a gun resounded through the air.

The lioness uttered a cry of pain and drew up one of her enormous paws, which had been pierced by the ball. But she was only wounded, and was dangerous still. Seeing this, I in my turn drew upon her. The ball crashed into her jaw, which fell useless. Thereupon the dogs flung themselves upon her flanks, and a terrible combat ensued.

A mute spectator of the fight, I dared not move. Another shot might have put an end to the sanguinary encounter, but the fear of wounding one of our dogs withheld my hand.

At length, seeing our faithful old dog Fan fall, rent from breast to flank by a blow from the lioness's paw, I no longer hesitated. Rushing forward, without thought of danger, I presented myself before the enraged beast. She raised herself upon her hind-legs to spring upon me, when I leaped forward and plunged my hunting-knife into her heart.

The noble beast, with a roar, rolled over upon the sand, never to rise again.

Fritz arrived upon the scene of action at once, forestalled only by a few minutes in the execution of an intention similar to my own.

For safety, I discharged a pistol into the head of the lion, and, feeling now quite secure, called Ernest and Jack.

They were already on the way to render us what assistance they could, for the moment they saw us in danger their fears vanished. They rushed into our arms, well-nigh overcome by excess of joy at finding us unhurt, after the great peril we had encountered.

The two lions lay extended upon the sand, and although we had nothing more to fear from them, we could not look upon their huge carcases without experiencing a sensation of terror.

The inanimate body of poor Fan lay stretched in death beside that of her huge enemy.

We had now been absent from Rock-house several days, and I knew that my wife would be getting anxious about us. Besides, our pearl-oysters, lying scattered upon the beach, were beginning to putrefy, and gave forth gases that were likely to prove injurious to our health. We determined, therefore, to return to the grotto, and to make the best of our way back again in a week or two, to take possession of the pearls which by that time, we felt sure, would be detached by decomposition from their fleshy beds.

We set out. Fritz, the sole occupant of his cajack, preceded us. When we were fairly outside the belt of rocks he approached the pirogue, and with the end of his paddle presented me with a letter, which he said, with a smile, "the postman had forgotten to deliver."

In order that I might give his brothers no cause for anxiety, I fell in with a pleasantry that had become familiar enough with us since the adventure of the carrier-pigeon, and withdrew to the stern of the boat to open the missive.

I was more troubled than surprised to learn that Fritz was about to quit us, in order to go in search of the unfortunate English girl who had written the message from the Burning Rock.

"Farewell, Fritz!" I cried. "Be prudent, and return as soon as you can, my dear son. Think of us and of your mother."

He kissed his hand from afar.

Four days later, I could not conceal my anxiety any longer, and proposed to set out in search of our fugitive.

After laying an abundant stock of provisions, and assuring ourselves that the pinnace, which we had not used for a long time, was in good condition, we set sail.

A fresh land breeze was blowing at the time, and our craft sped out to sea so swiftly that I was unable, for the time being, to manage it. On reaching the opening of the bay, it came into collision with a huge mass of something floating upon the water with so much force that it threw us all upon the deck. My wife and children uttered a cry of alarm. At the same moment we saw the floating mass send up into the air, with a tremendous hubbub, two great streams of water, and then plunge into the boiling and foaming sea.

We had come into collision with a spermaceti whale. The proximity of such a monster was by no means pleasant, and I laid our cannon ready to fire upon it. Ernest at once did his best to take accurate aim, and Jack fired off one of the pieces.

Our gunner had sighted his mark well. We saw the ball strike the monster full in the flank; and he at once buried himself in the depths, leaving a long trail of blood behind him, and making the sea boil again.

Some few moments afterwards he reappeared upon the surface. A second shot struck him in the head. He struggled violently for a time, and then, his strength failing him, he made for one of the rocks at the entrance to Deliverance Bay, and became stranded.

I was congratulating my son upon his skill and presence of mind, which had delivered us from so formidable an enemy, when all at once Jack cried out:

"A savage, father! a savage!"

We all looked in the direction indicated, and saw in the distance a strange canoe gliding over the waves with incredible swiftness.

The savage we fancied we had sighted seemed to have seen us, and to have at once disappeared behind a jutting rock.

The savage soon showed himself again, and seemed to examine us more attentively. Then he disappeared behind the promontory again, but only to reappear a few minutes afterwards.

Seeing that he continued to observe us, I took the speaking-trumpet, and, with all the strength of lung I could command, hailed him in the Malay language. He did not appear to understand me, for he still maintained his position.

"I fancy," said Jack, "that if we treat him to a few English sea-sayings, such as 'Shiver my timbers!' 'Lay-to, you lubbers!' 'Avast there!' and so on, he will the better comprehend our meaning."

Thereupon he laid hold of the speaking-trumpet, and carried out his intention.

Almost at the same moment the savage raised the branch of a tree above his head, in sign of peace, and began rowing swiftly in our direction.

The other boys laughed heartily at the success of Jack's device. But they soon changed their tone when they recognised in the savage, black as he was, and wearing a plume of feathers on his head, our dear Fritz.

In a short time he was upon the deck of the pinnace embracing us.

His mother, intoxicated with joy, overwhelmed him with kisses and caresses, without troubling herself about his strange costume or the colour of his skin.

It was not until we all burst into a laugh, on seeing her face disfigured with Fritz's war-paint, that she came to herself.

CHAPTER 30

Return of Fritz—Miss Jenny

I judged it wise now to tell my wife the secret of Fritz's expedition. Her surprise and, I am bound to add, her anxiety were extreme.

At length I asked Fritz to satisfy me upon two points. Had his expedition been successful? And to what end had he metamorphosed himself into a savage?

"My expedition has ended most satisfactorily," he replied, giving me a significant look; "and I cannot tell you how glad I am that I undertook it. As to my disguise, that was a measure of precaution. I saw you a long way off, and took you for Malay pirates. The reports of your cannon led me to think that you were in great force, and I therefore judged it prudent to change my garments and blacken my face, lest my European appearance should unduly attract your attention and curiosity."

My wife here interrupted us to wash Fritz's face. She soon restored him to his natural colour.

Leading Fritz apart, I asked him in a low voice to tell me what kind of a person it was that he had discovered; "Because," I added, "in some contingencies it would be better, perhaps, that you and I should go alone."

He reassured me in an instant.

"Father," he said, "I thought when I saw her that I was looking upon my mother at the age of fifteen, or rather, perhaps, upon one who should have been your daughter, if we had been granted the happiness of having a sister worthy of both her and you."

"Forward, then!" I cried, delighted. "Conduct us to the rock at once!"

Fritz immediately set out with amazing ardour and swiftness. Seated in his canoe, he shot ahead to guide us through the channels among the sunken rocks, and at length brought us to the far side of an island situated at the western end of Pearl Bay. A long tongue of land ran out into the sea, and formed a natural port, at which we landed.

Fritz leapt upon the beach without saying a word, and ran towards a clump of gigantic palms, among the umbrageous branches of which we descried a kind of hut, something like that at Falcon-nest, but constructed wholly of boughs. We naturally followed in the footsteps of our guide, and soon found ourselves standing before a fire composed of large stones, upon which was placed, in lieu of a pot, a large shell.

Fritz fired one of his pistols in the air, and at this signal we saw descending from a neighbouring tree, not a girl of fifteen as I had expected but a trim young sailor, slender in form, and of a modest and charming mien.

I know not how to describe the sensations we felt at this moment. For ten years the human race had been dead to us, and now all at once recollections of it were suddenly raised to life in the person of the fair creature standing before us. She looked almost a child, so beautiful and so ingenuous was her countenance.

We stood for an instant dazed and silent. My children, especially, could hardly believe their eyes. The stranger, upon her part, seemed to be equally undecided as to the line of conduct which she ought to pursue.

Fritz put an end to our embarrassment.

"My dear mother, dear father, and dear brothers," he said, "I present to you a friend—the young Lord Edward Montrose." At this point he looked at me significantly. "May he be welcomed as a son and a brother in our family circle!"

"He is welcome!" we all replied enthusiastically.

The young sailor looked so inexpressibly happy, that our sympathies were won over at once.

As head of the family I stepped forward, and, taking the stranger's hands in both my own, saluted her in the English manner, with as much warmth and kindness as if she had been one of my own sons, restored to us after a long separation.

I had understood from the look given me by Fritz, when he introduced the stranger as a man, that for the present he did not wish his brothers to know she was a girl. Both I and my wife kept the secret, and I desired the children to show their young comrade every hospitality.

My recommendation was needless. The young lord had already become the object of the most delicate attentions. Even the dogs greeted him with joy-barks and caresses.

Our supper was a joyous one. My boys, enlivened a little by some

Canary wine which I had brought out in honour of the occasion, gave free vent to their sprightliness; and we gossiped till a far later hour than usual.

After our guest had retired, Fritz proceeded to tell his brothers the story of his expedition, forgetting to substitute the name of Lord Edward for that of Miss Jenny. His delighted listeners could hardly wait to meet their new sister.

The next morning they met her with an air half of embarrassment and half of mischief, and saluted her by the name of Miss Jenny. The poor child blushed and lowered her eyes at first, but, recovering herself almost instantly, she frankly held out her hand to the young monkeys, and with charming grace commended herself to their brotherly friendship.

After breakfast—which, thanks to some chocolate prepared by Fritz, was a very substantial one—we determined to set sail, in order to recover what remained of the whale we had killed on the previous day.

We cut the monster up as best we could, and by the advice of Jenny—who saw clearly enough that, circumstanced as we were, a half-loaf was better than no bread—we determined to take away at once as much blubber as we could put in our sacks and stow away in the pinnace, and leave the rest to the vultures.

When this labour came to an end we returned to Burning Rock, to bring away the baggage of the young Englishwoman, and then, after bidding adieu to the island, and christening the creek where Fritz had landed by the name of Happy Bay, on account of our fortunate discovery of Miss Jenny, we set out for Pearl Bay, where it was necessary to make a short sojourn before returning to Rock-house.

On arriving there we found that the lions had become a prey to vultures and other birds, and that nothing was left of them but a few bones bleaching in the sand. We put up our tent, intending to stay only as long as was necessary to harvest our pearls from the shells of the decomposed fish. But a discovery which I made delayed our departure.

Among the rocks, I remarked one which appeared to be calcareous or chalky, and I thereupon determined to build a kiln, and endeavour to prepare some lime.

We set vigorously to work. The kiln was built and filled with chalk, and a fire was lighted above and below, which it was necessary to leave burning for several days.

During this operation we had plenty of leisure on our hands, and, being pressed by his brothers, Fritz set apart a portion of each evening, after Miss Jenny had retired to rest, to recount his adventures in search of Burning Rock. He began his narrative as follows:

"You remember the circumstances under which I left you, after handing our father a letter, in which I explained to him the object of my excursion. Well, on setting out the sea was calm and the weather fine, but I had no sooner passed Pearl Bay than a terrible tempest arose. My cajack not being strong enough to do battle with the waves, I allowed it to float at will.

"But I was far from any point that I could recognise. The country around me was different to anything I had yet seen. The coasts of the islands among which I found myself were fringed with enormous rocks whose points pierced the clouds, while inland I could see gigantic forests, in which birds of varied and brilliant plumage flew from bough to bough, and majestic rivers that roared down to the sea.

"After a journey of some hours, the face of the coast changed, and I found myself opposite scenery of a far more pastoral character. The songs of inoffensive birds alone broke the silence of the peaceful-looking solitude. I landed in perfect security, and, having fastened my boat to a large boulder, made a hearty meal of oysters and other shell-fish, which I found lying in large quantities along the beach.

"By this time day was on the wane, and, as I did not think it prudent to pass the night in a region so altogether unknown to me, I determined to sleep in my cajack. I anchored the craft a few fathoms out, by tying a large stone to a rope fastened to the prow, and throwing it into the water.

"The next morning I again set out on my voyage. My cajack cut through the waves like an arrow and I abandoned myself to the enjoyment of the magnificent scenery that lay spread out before me.

"Towards noon, fatigued by several hours of continual rowing, I decided to land near a little wood, the aspect of which was most inviting. The luxuriant foliage of the trees was peopled with humming-birds, paroquets, and a thousand other feathered songsters, who kept up a continuous and harmonious concert. At once surprised and delighted, I pushed on beneath overhanging bowers, formed of branches and trailing plants, which stretched from tree to tree, and dropped in graceful festoons almost to my head.

"I unhooded my eagle, who, feeling himself free, took wing, and soon returned with a little paroquet, which I took away and was examining, when all at once I heard behind me a crackling among the branches, as if some large animal were making its way through them.

"I turned round, and what think you I saw? A huge striped tiger, not more than ten or twelve paces away from me! I saw at once that it was too late to think of flight. I was so terrified that I could hardly hold my gun, which, besides, would be but a feeble protection against so redoubtable an enemy.

"A cold perspiration broke from every pore in my body, and I verily believed that my last hour was come; when suddenly my eagle, who no doubt well understood the danger in which I was placed, precipitated himself upon the head of the tiger, and with beak and claws began to tear out its eyes.

"I was saved! The tiger, fully occupied in defending itself against the furious attack of the bird, took no further notice of me. Seeing this, I approached, drew my pistols, and fired them. One shot crashed into the creature's skull: he uttered a terrific roar and fell over dead.

"The joy which I felt on achieving this victory was tempered, however, by a most poignant grief. One of my shots, aimed hastily, had struck the eagle, which fell dead at the same moment as the tiger. I took the faithful bird up, and, weeping tears of regret, carried it down to the cajack, to be brought home and preserved in our museum.

"Quitting this place sad at heart, without even staying to skin the tiger, I rowed away listlessly, overcome by disappointment. Indeed, I was just upon the point of tacking about, in order to return to Rock-house, when, among the peaks of a small rocky island to my right, I saw a thin wreath of fiery smoke curling slowly up towards the sky.

"'The Burning Rock!' I cried, lifting my hands to heaven in an attitude of devour thankfulness.

"My ardour at once returned. I laid on to my oars with all my might and in a short time effected a landing, not without some risk, upon the rocky coast of the island.

"I managed to climb with difficulty, using both my hands and my feet, to the top of a rock, whence I hoped to be able to survey the whole island. After looking about me for an instant, I followed a narrow pathway which led me down to a sort of platform, some few yards square, sheltered on all sides by the neighbouring rocks.

"Arrived there, I cautiously approached the entrance to a large cavern, which I thought perhaps might be the lair of some beast of prey. I was walking on tiptoe, with my pistols in my hand and my eyes and ears on the alert, when, through a break in the rocks, I perceived, with an emotion I cannot describe to you, a human creature, dressed like a man, but bearing every appearance of being a young girl, lying asleep, with her head resting on her arm, upon a bed of moss and dried leaves. I stood immovable and speechless. My surprise was as great as if the discovery, which had been the sole object of my expedition, were wholly unexpected. For the first time during ten years I was looking upon a human creature who was not one of our own family!

"I hardly dared breathe. I stood gazing steadfastly upon the sleeping castaway. My joy was extreme to find that, instead of some poor creature worn out with age and fatigue, I was to rescue a young and charming girl. The features of the sleeper wore an expression so altogether infantine, that I did not think she could be more than twelve or fourteen years old. Her costume was that of a young midshipman. Long light hair fell about her face and upon her neck, and her little hand peeped out from among a mass of ringlets.

"I thanked God that he had chosen me to be the means of rescuing this lovely creature, and of presenting to my father and mother so beautiful a daughter, and to my brothers so amiable a sister. Her costume, after I had once examined her features, did not deceive me for an instant. Francis himself, who was so beautiful in his infancy, had not a softer or more delicate skin. I could only compare her to what I supposed our mother to have been at her age.

"A thousand confused thoughts agitated my mind. I would have given anything could my mother have stood in my place, so that the fair stranger on awaking might have looked upon first her sweet face. I might have stood there dreaming I know not how long, but that a little bird, untroubled by scruples like my own, skimmed noisily into the cavern and posted himself upon the fair young sleeper's forehead.

"Waking with a start, she raised herself into a sitting posture, and peered round with her large lustrous eyes to see what it was that had disturbed her repose. The real offender had flown, and her eyes rested upon me.

"She uttered a cry of mingled surprise and terror.

"With a gesture almost of supplication, I strove to calm her, 'Fear nothing,' I said; 'I am far more alarmed than you are, and do not intend you any harm.'

"'Who are you?' she asked. 'Whence come you? How did you get here?'

"Then leaping lightly to her feet—

"'Whoever you are,' she said, 'so that you be an honest man, I bid you welcome to this solitude.'

"'I am,' I replied, 'the unknown knight to whom you appealed by the message which you confided to the care of the albatross. I have quitted all to come to your rescue. I am not an Englishman, as you may tell by my accent, but I am a citizen of a free country, where we know the respect which is due to misfortune. A tempest, no doubt, cast you upon this rock. A tempest cast me and my father and mother and three brothers upon a neighbouring island. Ten years have we been separated from the rest of mankind, dwelling upon a corner of the earth which has now become our world. If you can put confidence in me, I will conduct you to my family.'

"'Heaven reward you!' she said in a voice broken by emotion—'you and yours! you have rescued me from a life that was worse than death, from a solitude that was fast becoming unbearable. If your father and mother will not turn me from their door, I shall strive to become the most grateful and submissive of daughters.'

"The similarity of our misfortunes soon established a perfect confidence between us. Miss Jenny—this, she said, was her name—told me that she had been cast half dead upon the rock where I found her; and, once there, she had achieved miracles of courage, of patience, and of industry to find the wherewithal to satisfy the first cravings of nature.

"Thanks to the provisions with which dear mother had furnished the cajack, I was enabled to lay before my new-found friend a supper which she pronounced exquisite.

"We then retired for the night—I to my cajack, she to her hut in the tree, to which she climbed with the agility of a squirrel.

"In the morning I used every effort to induce the young lady to take one of the seats in the cajack, and return with me to Rock-house; but she resolutely refused to leave behind her the thousand little objects which she had either made or found, and applied to useful purposes in her solitude.

"I therefore set out alone, with the double purpose of procuring a larger vessel and of bringing my mother to give the poor stranger a maternal welcome.

"It was while on my way to Rock-house, with these objects in view, that I sighted the pinnace, and, taking you for pirates, disguised myself as you saw."

CHAPTER 31

The History of Miss Jenny—A Family Feast—Musical Recreations

On the following morning, after breakfast, Ernest, Jack and Francis took possession of their eldest brother, and begged him to continue the history of our young friend, who was too shy to recount it herself.

This, in brief, was the story:—

Sir William Montrose, a major in the British army, had obtained the command of an important post in India, and went out there. While fulfilling his command he lost his wife, and was left with an only daughter, scarcely seven years of age—Miss Jenny. He lavished all his affection upon the little one thus committed to his charge, undertaking her education himself, and wisely determining so to train her that in the event of any reverse of fortune, she might be able to confront peril bravely, and do battle with adversity. Miss Jenny's natural aptitude rendered his task easy of accomplishment. At fifteen years of age she was as clever in the management of a gun or a horse as she was fitted to move with ease and good breeding in the best society.

A circumstance now occurred which for the first time separated the father and daughter. Sir William was promoted, and named commander of an expedition destined for a distant part of the country. Not being able to take his daughter with him, he confided her to the care of a friend, the captain of a British war-vessel, who undertook to convey her to England, and place her in charge of one of Sir William's sisters, who was childless. At the end of a year the father hoped to bring his expedition to an end, when he proposed to obtain leave of absence and rejoin his daughter in London.

The young lady embarked in the costume of a midshipman, because women were not allowed to travel on board a man-of-war.

The voyage was a prosperous one during the first few days; but after that a terrible tempest arose, which drove the ship leagues out of her course, and eventually carried her to the same coast where we ourselves had been wrecked ten years before. Having struck upon the rocks, the vessel broke her back and foundered. One boat alone could be put to sea. In it was placed Miss Jenny and as many of the officers and men as it would hold, lots being cast to select those who were to take this last chance of deliverance. Hardly had the frail craft received its living freight, when a huge wave struck and capsized it. By a miracle almost, the young girl, who had become insensible, was carried on the crests of the breakers to the top of a rock on the volcanic island, where we found her. She saw no more of the men, some thirty in number, who had embarked with her in the boat.

The first days of solitude were full of horror for the unfortunate young castaway. Thrown upon an unknown coast, she had little in prospect beyond a slow death by starvation, or a quicker one by the attack of some terrible beast of prey. How happy to her now was the reflection that she had received an education which had developed in her courage, fortitude, and ingenuity—qualities so necessary in the new mode of life she was about to commence!

She at once set about constructing a hut, or rather a nest, in the trees as we had done ourselves at Falcon-nest. Hunting and fishing supplied her with food. Among the few pieces of wreck washed up by the tide, she found some nails, which she bent and used as fish-hooks, plaiting threads drawn from her garments to serve as lines. With the larger iron-work thrown up she made a number of crude tools for daily use, and weapons for her defence against unknown enemies. She was thus enabled to cut out arrows, which she used with great adroitness in her hunting excursions. Her food, however, consisted chiefly of fruits, shell-fish, roots, and dried fish—especially during the rainy season, which had reduced her to the most terrible privation.

One of her favourite pastimes had been to catch young birds, which she tamed and trained. It was thus that she had obtained the albatross, which, after involuntarily delivering her message to Fritz, had faithfully carried my son's reply back again.

Such, in a few words, was the story Fritz had to tell us.

By sunset the pinnace was loaded with everything that we intended to carry with us.

We desired much to return to Rock-house, my sons especially, for they were impatient to do the honours of the establishment to their young companion.

They had painted for her a picture of our island home so enchanting, that when we raised anchor in the morning she could not restrain a cry of joy.

On nearing Deliverance Bay, and seeing Cape Disappointment

in the distance, I proposed to sail on to Prospect Hill, to ascertain whether the farmery was still in good condition. Fritz and Francis, who preceded us in the cajack, went straight to Rock-house to prepare for our reception.

The two young men, who had gone on before, had, as I expected, used every effort to receive us with distinction. Our approach to the entrance of Deliverance Bay was signalised by two rounds of ordnance, to which I replied with the guns of the pinnace.

As we doubled the cape of Shark Island, we saw Fritz and Francis in the cajack, coming to meet us. Once in sight, they tacked about, and piloted us to land. When we had cast anchor Fritz leapt ashore, and with imperturbable gravity announced himself as the Governor of the Castle of Rock-house, to which mansion he invited us, to partake of the refreshments there awaiting our arrival. Then with knightly courtesy, he offered his hand to Miss Jenny, and conducted her to the umbrageous verandah in front of our grotto.

In the open air, in front of the door, we saw with surprise a table laid out with all the choicest productions of the island. The calabash dishes were filled with magnificent ananas, intermingled with fresh green leaves; while pyramids of oranges stood side by side with baskets of figs and guavas. Canary wine, hydromel, and fresh milk from our cows invited us temptingly to slake our thirst. In the centre of the table lay a couple of roasted fowls and a dish of fried fish. Over the table was suspended a double garland of leaves, on which were picked out in flower-blooms these words:

"A thousand welcomes to our dear sister Jenny! May the day be long remembered on which she first set foot in the dwelling of the Swiss Robinson!"

Miss Jenny took her place between my wife and me: it was only right that she should occupy the seat of honour. Ernest and Jack faced us. Fritz and Francis would not sit down at all. Napkin on arm, like waiters at an hotel, they ran hither and thither, cut the joints, changed the plates, poured out wine, with a gravity and agility which was as admirable as it was droll.

The afternoon was made a complete holiday. Each of the boys did his best to entertain our young guest. She was taken all over the grotto and all over the adjacent ground.

The next morning early, the whole household was afoot, for we had determined to make an excursion to Falcon-nest, with the exception of Miss Jenny, who was still weak in health, and to whom therefore Jack lent his buffalo: we all went on foot.

The house in the tree had again suffered from the weather, and we all set to work to restore it. Three days sufficed to put it into habitable condition.

While we were engaged in this labour, a few showers of rain fell, and warned us to gather in our harvest and stores of provisions for the winter.

In these latter occupations Miss Jenny displayed an amount of ingenuity and willingness which rendered her aid invaluable to us. She did my wife a thousand nameless services, and crept deeper into her love every day. We all worked so vigorously, that we had nothing to fear when the rainy season set in.

Miss Jenny perfected us in the pronunciation of the English language. Fritz and Ernest, if I may trust her report, acquired as pure an accent as a born Englishman. On her part, she learnt in a very short time to speak German with a charming accuracy, and even with grace; and this, to my wife, was an accomplishment which she could never find words to praise sufficiently.

The union between the two women was perfect—so much so that when, one day, Jenny asked in a voice trembling with apprehension whether she might be permitted to call my dear wife by the sacred name of "mother", her only answer was a passionate burst of tears and a warm maternal embrace. It was a touching scene, awaking emotions known only to the hearts of those who love each other tenderly.

"Once more, then," cried Jenny, weeping for joy, "I have a mother—a beautiful and loving mother."

"And I," said my wife, not less moved, "have found a charming daughter, as good as she is brave and courageous," and she took Jenny to her heart.

Jenny had a remarkable voice, and a rare talent for music. Her memory, also, was such that she knew by heart the choicest *morceaux* from all the greater masters. She not only charmed our solitude by her singing, but she taught Francis, who had great aptitude in that direction.

For the first time the sun reappeared without finding us bemoaning his absence.

CHAPTER 32

A Grave Incident—On the Look-out—Visitors—New Friends

Notwithstanding all the charms of our enforced solicitude my sons felt, as the fine season again approached, an insatiable desire for liberty and independence. They left the grotto as birds escape from their cages, flying on swiftest wing to fields bathed in light.

Fritz, the intrepid sailor, proposed to make an excursion to Shark Island, for the purpose of ascertaining whether the sea, during its tumult, had thrown anything valuable upon the rocks. As I could not accompany him, he set out with Jack.

I desired them, in accordance with our invariable custom at the end of the rainy season, to fire off two rounds of ordnance on their arrival at their destination. We had a double purpose in pursuing this course. The guns would serve as a signal to any poor creature who might have been wrecked upon our coasts, and also it would enable us to establish communications with any vessel that might find itself in our neighbourhood.

But what was their astonishment when they distinctly heard, far out at sea, the report of a gun in response to their double detonation!

At first they were in doubt, thinking it an echo; but in a short time the first report was succeeded by another. Some minutes after, while they were listening in silent anxiety, a third report resounded over the waves.

Without more ado they leapt into the cajack, which, impelled by two pairs of vigorous arms, literally flew across to the beach.

"What has happened?" I asked, seeing their scared look.

Then they imparted their astonishing news.

At first I thought they had been deceived; but they affirmed so energetically and so seriously that they had distinctly heard three cannon-shots, that it was impossible for me any longer to doubt the fact. But were we to rejoice or to be alarmed? Had we in our neighbourhood Europeans or Malay pirates? Such were the grave questions I asked myself.

I hastened to assemble the family and take counsel with them, for I found the subject too grave to decide upon myself.

Darkness surprised us before we had come to a conclusion. I gave the signal to retire to rest, advising my boys to keep watch by turns during the night in front of the grotto, lest we should be surprised.

The weather was lovely at first, but later on a terrible storm arose. The rain fell in torrents, and the howling of the wind and the dash of the waves prevented us hearing any other sound seaward.

During two days and two nights, it seemed as if the rainy season had recommenced. It was quite impossible for us to go out, as we intended, to take observations.

On the third day the wind fell, the sea became calm, and we were able to make a voyage to Shark Island. I went thither with Fritz, taking with me a couple of flags, with which to make signals either of joy or alarm to our dear ones who remained at home at Rock-house.

If I lowered the flag three times and finally cast it into the sea, they were to take instant flight to Falcon-nest. If, on the contrary, I waved it over my head, they were to remain where they were and fear nothing.

You may imagine with what beating hearts we landed and climbed to our observatory. We swept the horizon carefully on all sides with our telescopes, and, discovering nothing, I told Fritz to charge and fire the cannon.

He obeyed me, and a few minutes afterwards we heard, in the direction of the south-west, which we had never explored, first one report, then a second, then a third, and so on, to the seventh report.

We had no doubt whatever now that there was a vessel in our neighbourhood.

We returned to the family without having given them a signal.

I told them that I had determined to set out on a voyage of discovery, in company with Fritz, and this project had their unanimous assent. Jenny, indeed, ordinarily so calm and business-like, gave expression to the wildest hopes. She was certain, she said, that the strange ship could belong to no one but her father, who, having returned to London and heard of the wreck, had set out instantly in search of his lost daughter.

I had all the provisions put in safety, and as Fritz and I set out in the cajack, my wife, Miss Jenny, and my three younger sons departed for Falcon-nest, taking with them the cattle.

Utilising the idea which Fritz had hit upon some months before, we disguised ourselves as savages, thinking that, in any case, this device would lay us less open to suspicion as to our intentions. This, however, did not prevent us from concealing our best arms in the bottom of the canoe.

It was near upon mid-day when we set sail, and more than an hour elapsed before we rounded the western cape of Deliverance Bay.

After rowing straight on for something like three hours in waters quite unknown to us, we found ourselves under a cape, which we determined to double by coasting, so that while we saw everything before us, we might be seen as little as possible.

Judge of our astonishment when, on rounding the promontory, we saw lying at anchor in the bay behind it a large three-master, flying the English flag.

A little distance up the beach a large tent was erected, and a fire was burning, before which some joints of meat were in process of roasting. The crew of the ship appeared to be very numerous. Two sentinels were pacing backwards and forwards on the deck. We ventured out of our concealment, whereupon one of them disappeared, and quickly returned with an officer, who held a telescope under his arm.

"That is the captain," said Fritz. "I recognise him by his uniform. We have nothing to fear, father, for his features are undoubtedly those of a European."

Taking up the speaking-trumpet, I shouted with all my might in English—"Englishmen! Good men!" without adding anything else.

The captain, who evidently took us for the savages we appeared to be, made signs to us to advance, at the same time displaying before us some pieces of red cloth, together with axes, nails, beads, and other articles which it is usual to exchange with the indigenous inhabitants of the New World.

His mistake caused us a good deal of amusement; but we were not yet satisfied that we should be safe in putting ourselves in his power.

We consequently determined to go away, and to present ourselves on the morrow in our proper persons, and with more pomp before our European visitors.

We made signs of farewell, and disappeared briskly behind the promontory.

Joy had doubled our strength, and in a very short time we were again with our family, who awaited us with impatience.

We employed the remainder of the day in putting the armament of our craft in order, in bedecking her gaily with flags, and in the preparation of the old uniforms which we had brought off the wreck ten years before. We also laid in a stock of our choicest fruits and the principal productions of our islands, which we intended to present to the captain; for we judged it wise to inspire him and his crew with an exaggerated idea of our wealth and power.

Next morning after breakfast we lifted anchor. Near the guns, which were loaded, stood Jack and Ernest. Fritz, in the uniform of a naval officer, preceded us in the cajack.

I ordered the British flag to be hoisted, and in a few moments it was floating gaily out to the winds from the foremast of the pinnace.

The astonishment of the English crew on seeing a vessel with flags flying and all sails set, advancing proudly into the bay, was so great, that if we had been pirates I verily believe we should have been able to make an easy prize of the ship in the first moments of confusion which our appearance had brought about among her crew.

Having taken in sail at some distance from the vessel, I and Fritz embarked in the pinnace's boat, which we towed behind us, and rowed on to salute the captain, who from the quarter-deck replied to us most amicably, and invited us on board without delay.

The worthy officer received us with all a sailor's frankness and cordiality, and leading us into his cabin, inviting us to drink a flagon of old port with him, asked us under what circumstances it was that we found ourselves upon an island which, as he had understood, was only inhabited by savages.

I briefly narrated to him the history of our shipwreck, and of our life upon the island. I also spoke to him of Miss Jenny, and asked if he had ever chanced to hear of her father, Sir William Montrose.

He said he knew the name of the gentleman well, and had heard that after distinguishing himself in his expedition in India, he had returned to England, and retired from the service. As for himself, his name was Littlestone, and he was commander of the frigate *Unicorn*. Overtaken by a storm, he had been driven out of his course, but had been fortunate enough to find an excellent port at a moment when he had almost given his vessel up for lost. As the parts in which he found himself were wholly unknown to him, he thought perhaps I could give him some information which would be of value.

When the captain had finished speaking, I begged him to do me the honour of paying a visit to the pinnace, in order that I might present him to my family.

He at once accepted my invitation, and embarking in one of his own boats, which was rowed by two of his sailors, was soon on board our vessel. It is unnecessary to say that he was received with every manifestation of joy. Miss Jenny, especially, displayed the liveliest satisfaction at being able to speak of her father to a compatriot.

The captain had among his passengers an English family, whose acquaintance we were happy enough to make. It consisted of Mr. Woolton, a distinguished engineer and shipbuilder, whose health had suffered much during the voyage; his wife, Mrs. Woolton; and their two charming daughters, one aged fourteen and the other twelve. Notwithstanding the tenderest attentions of his wife and children, Mr. Woolton had been growing feebler and feebler daily. The sea-air was too bracing for him, and to save his life it was necessary that he should land as soon as possible. We offered him and his family an asylum at Rock-house, placing at their service everything in our possession.

Our proposition was accepted with gratitude, and the same day the amiable family was transferred to our island home.

The surprise with which the newcomers surveyed our possessions would be difficult to express. Their exclamations of astonishment, repeated enthusiastically over every object that met their view, amused my sons hugely. They could hardly bring themselves to believe that six persons had been able to achieve so much by their own unaided exertions. In the evening we took supper under the verandah, and until bed-time conversed together with gaiety and animation.

During the night my wife and I were occupied by the gravest thoughts. The opportunity we had so long prayed for, of returning to our friends in Europe, had at last offered itself. Should we profit by it? Why, we asked ourselves after reflection—why should we abandon a home where we had been so happy, with the object of renewing relations which time and absence had probably destroyed for ever? Had we not reached an age when tranquillity and repose were far more pleasing to us than the risk of a voyage to the Eastern Hemisphere? Nevertheless, we had no desire that our own decision should influence that of our sons, if they wished to return to their fatherland—though the idea of parting from them rent our hearts.

Miss Jenny, since she had learned that her father was in England, ardently desired to go thither and rejoin him.

I doubted not that her departure would be the cause of deep grief to my eldest son, who had never concealed the profound affection which the young girl had inspired in him.

The next morning, at breakfast, Mr. Woolton, who already felt the better for his brief sojourn on land, gave me his hand and said: "The life which you lead in this solitude pleases me immensely. I feel that I should grow young again in this magnificent country, and I should esteem myself fortunate if I could obtain your consent to take up my habitation in some corner of it."

The proposition was received with joy. We all of us expressed the happiness we should have in admitting him to our colony with his wife and daughters. I also took advantage of the occasion to announce that I and my wife had come to the resolution to end our days in that beautiful island—to which I desired to give the name of "New Switzerland".

"To the prosperity of New Switzerland!" cried the whole party, raising their calabash vessels filled with palm-wine.

"And long life and prosperity to all who dwell in it!" added Ernest, Jack, and Francis.

I remarked that Fritz kept silence, from which circumstance I understood that he secretly wished to accompany Miss Jenny. The poor boy hoped, no doubt, that her father would consent to her union with one who had been the means of rescuing her from her cruel solitude.

Jenny approached me. "My father," she said, in a voice broken by emotion—and it was the first time she had called me by this name—"My father, bestow upon me your blessing as my mother has done; let me—let *us* go. We shall come again to see you. Do not think that we are about to part from you for ever. Sir William Montrose is a man of honour and of the tenderest heart. He will certainly discharge his daughter's obligations when he knows that his daughter's happiness depends upon his doing so. He returned to Europe on my account, and on mine alone; he will quit Europe for my sake and for yours." Then, looking tenderly at Fritz—"Have confidence in us both," she said; "Fritz will answer for me, and I, knowing him as I do, will answer for him."

I embraced the noble child.

My wife gave her consent.

I gave mine.

Fritz, distracted by joy and grief, embraced first one and then the other, laughing and weeping by turns.

"Rest assured, dear father," he said on leaving us, "your son will always do his duty. I shall not be worthy of success if I am not prepared for reverses."

I have little to add. A year had not passed away before all that our charming young prophetess had predicted had come to pass, with one exception.

Her father was dead before she reached London, and she had not the consolation of seeing him again.

Five years have passed since then, and what changes have taken place! The sailors of the *Unicorn*, on their arrival in Europe, spread the account of our history in every land. The wealth at our disposal in the natural resources of the island was said to be almost unlimited. In a little while these stories produced their natural results, and the tide of emigration began to flow in the direction of this remote place. The settlers had not been attracted to a barren spot. The island contained abundant resources for the support of a large colony, and as those who came out were for the most part not wanting in energy, they soon found themselves provided with the necessaries of life. The population rapidly increased; and at the present hour we number more than two thousand souls.

Ernest and Jack are wedded to the two amiable daughters of Mr. Woolton.

Jack followed the trade of a shipbuilder, and is at the head of a considerable establishment, organized under the superintendence of his father-in-law.

A more splendid destiny seems to be reserved for Ernest. He was always of an adventurous character, and, young as he is, he has already returned from his second voyage to Europe.

Francis, "little" no longer, and handsome as well as tall and stout-built, is captain of a merchantman.

My dear wife and I are old, no doubt—at least we are bound to believe it when we consult our mirror, though, thank Heaven, we find no special intimation of the fact in our hearts. The freshness of feeling of our youth has been permitted to remain with us, and in caressing our children's children we seem to forget the time that has passed away since we fondled our own. Our sons, too, are still our "boys". It is an unspeakable pride to us to see them all doing well in the world; industrious, handsome to look upon, content with their lot.

And when the time shall come for us to render up our souls to the Sovereign Lord of all, we shall be found ready. The grand voyage—that which leads us to God—has no anxieties for those who during their whole lives have served and honoured Him.